Fever Pitz

Joseph Curry

First published by Mogzilla in 2020.

Paperback edition:
ISBN: 9781906132361

www.mogzilla.co.uk

Printed in the UK

For Esther, Owen and Aidan

Chapter One

A Game For The Gods

Brightness stood before the temple with the heavy rubber ball in her hands, the brilliant yellow feathers of her headdress fluttering in the gentle breeze. Surrounding the court, the crowd fell silent as her father, their king, addressed them.

"Today, we play this game in honour of the gods. In the great war that will arrive in the days to come, we will need their guidance, their love and their strength."

He stood tall, his dark eyes glowing with pride, his bronzed face partially hidden by ink patterns and the large jade shells he wore on his nose and ears, his body covered in a mixture of bright blue and jet-black paint.

"My name is Blazing Sky," he said. "I rule this city. My father ruled this city before me and his father before him. My son will rule when my bones are in the ground."

His voice was bold but calm and he continued.

"A great storm approaches our people and we must be strong. Do not let yourself become strangled by fear. Dismiss it from your hearts. Fight for me and this city if you wish but more than anything fight for yourselves. Fight those that will seek to burn your homes to the ground, steal your possessions and kill your children. I call upon the gods to guide us and lead us to victory."

Brightness watched as the King raised his hand and the crowds came to life, roaring in defiant fury. The sound of horns rang out, echoing around the whole court. It was time for the game to begin.

Holding the heavy rubber ball, made from Cau-ucho trees, in her hands, Brightness stole a glance at her older brother who stood opposite her. She and Sunfire had played Pitz almost since the day they learned to walk and there were no finer players within the walls of a city in which the game was of great importance, with just about every man, woman and child packed into the ball court. Some watched from rows of stone seats whereas others managed to view the spectacle from higher vantage points.

Many times, Brightness had taken to the court at her brother's side, often bringing honour to the city by defeating rivals. Today, their father had decided that they would be opponents for the first time, the two best players in the city, both only having ever lost a single game and that being to the famous twins of Tikal, the very city that now prepared to attack them. The gods would want to see this he had told her and at this grave time they should do all they could to please them. Their future depended on it.

Throwing the ball up into the air, she allowed it to drop before bringing her forearm rapidly forward and striking it with her protective padding so that it sailed upwards and into the opposite side of the court. Immediately, she watched Sunfire react, covering the ground as quickly as ever with his powerful, muscular legs, his jaguar headdress giving the impression of a wild predator pouncing on its prey. Sliding on the stone floor, he flexed his hip at the ball, flicking it up for a team-mate to strike it back across the middle line of the court and back into Brightness' path. Such was the ferocity of the strike, it drew an audible cry from the crowd. Diving to her right, she managed to deflect the ball upwards with her leg, ignoring the throbbing pain this caused her and jumping quickly back to her feet. Seeing her partner, Flint-Knife, move into position and strike the ball upwards with his hip, she jumped as high as she could so she was above it before swinging her padded knee violently downwards.

Despite a valiant effort, this time Sunfire could not make an interception, the ball escaping his desperate lunge and bouncing off the stone floor. Brightness had won the first point of the game and the whole court seemed to vibrate with energy as people cheered or cursed with equal intensity. She knew that many of them would have bet on the outcome, wagering anything from precious jewels to beautiful, rare feathers. It wasn't unknown for someone to sell themselves into slavery to pay off the debts that they had accumulated.

"Very good Princess," Flint-Knife told her, the eyes of his handsome face twinkling a little. "I can see that I may rest my bones today and leave the hard work to you."

Brightness smiled. She was used to her partner's gentle teasing.

"You will do your share," she answered. "Or my father will bring you before the nobles and have you punished."

Brightness watched her brother rise to his feet a little gingerly. Landing on the hard, stone surface had knocked the wind out of him but they both knew that in this game suffering an injury was inevitable. The very least you could expect were a few nasty bruises. Brightness had suffered far worse during the last few years. Although as a player of Pitz, she wore protective padding on her knees, forearms, hips and head, she'd still broken bones in both her elbows as well as cracking her cheekbone. If the heavy ball struck you in the wrong place, it could do serious damage or even cause death. She had little time for such thoughts as Sunfire restarted the game by sending the ball soaring into the air. Flint-knife, studying the flight carefully, positioned himself beneath it. The rules of the game dictated that the ball must not strike the ground within your area of the court, so thrusting his right hip upwards, he controlled it so that it floated just a little way above Brightness's head. Trying her best to ignore the distraction of the crowd's wild shrieking, she bounced the ball off her shoulder pad, sending it across the centre line and into her opponents' half. This time, Sunfire allowed his partner to intercept the ball. Skilfully, the young man let it deflect off the outside of his knee towards the far side of the court where Sunfire was now poised and ready and at the last moment Brightness realised what her brother was going to do. The ball game was due to last until the last rays of sunlight had disappeared, with players exhausted by the end of play. Whichever team had won the most points by then was declared the winner. There was only one thing that would change this. High up above the two parallel sloping walls that stood at the side of the court, was a large stone ring. A player who managed to get the ball to pass through it would shower themselves in glory but a shot such as this was extremely rare to achieve considering the difficulty involved. A player who attempted this game-winning feat would also risk automatically conceding the point if they, as was usually the case, missed their target. This type of play was usually reserved for desperate teams who were resigned to losing on points. In all the years, she'd played and watched the game of Pitz, Brightness had only ever seen anyone make this shot on one or two occasions. Most attempts didn't get particularly close and to try this so early in the game was unusual as it was more common for players to wait until they were far enough in front that they could afford to relinquish a point, or far enough behind their opponents that only this shot could save the game. If anything, it angered Brightness a little to see her brother take aim at the stone ring. By doing so, he was sending the message that he wasn't worried about falling behind a few points early on in the game, so confident he was that he was good enough to recover the deficit.

Holding her breath, she watched Sunfire thrust his hip into the rubber ball. There was nothing she could do now but wait and hope. For hours, she'd practised striking the ball through the stone hoop with her brother and occasionally he'd managed to pull off this feat. However, it was one thing doing it when they had the court to themselves and quite another to carry it out during the frenzy of competition. The ball sailed upwards, the crowd whooping and hollering with excitement as they realised Sunfire's intentions. To Brightness's relief, for the humiliation of such a quick defeat would have been unbearable, it missed the target narrowly, crashing off the bottom corner of the ring and bouncing down to the ground. She took a deep breath. Another point had been won but this was only the beginning. If she was going to beat her older brother, she would have to work for it. He would never give in.

Chapter Two

The Eyes Of A Snake

The game proved to be every bit as difficult as
Brightness had imagined. In stifling heat, her legs
became more leaden with every leap, stretch and step
that she made, while her body ached from the bumps
and bruises suffered when diving for the ball on the
solid surface. With the sun beginning to drop, her early
lead had melted away with Sunfire and his partner
recovering from their early setback to establish a
narrow lead. Her forehead glistening with sweat, she
leapt to her right once more, successfully preventing the
ball from striking the ground and trying not to wince
from the pain she felt as she landed with a loud thud.
She was on her feet in a flash, summoning the energy to
spring to her feet in time to watch Flint-Knife striking
the ball into the opposite side of the court.

If Sunfire was tiring, he was keeping the signs
hidden. Moving backwards to position his feet for a
high ball, he flicked it up with his knee and into his
team-mate's path. Propelling the heavy ball forward
with his forearm, the young man hit it towards
Brightness with such power that she didn't have time
to set her feet and react. To her horror, she realised
that the ball was going to strike her in the face and she
gasped in spite of herself. A broken jaw or shattered
cheekbone was the least she could expect. A fleeting
memory of the mangled face of a previous opponent
flickered within her mind. Sunfire had hit him with

a powerful strike, leaving his nose a bloody mess of flesh and shattered bone, his left eye socket smashed to pieces. Although she'd suffered many injuries herself, the thought of her face being damaged beyond repair frightened her.

Her breath trapped within her throat and trying in vain to lift a hand for protection, she braced herself for the impact and the crushing pain that would surely follow, but with the ball no more than a finger's length from her nose, she became aware of feet pounding across the stone to her left. It was as if time itself had slowed down with every sound and movement more acute. Brightness was aware of the sea of faces surrounding the court, their eyes wide with shock, each seeming to scream out a warning. Then, at the last moment, the athletic figure of Flint-Knife came into vision, hurling his body into the ball's path with a desperate leap

With a sickening crunch, the ball struck him in the rib cage before he landed on the floor with a thud, the side of his head ricocheting off the stone. Frozen to the spot, Brightness watched as he lay motionless, the crowd falling silent momentarily as they leant in, trying to get a better view of the stricken player. Sunfire was at his side in an instant, turning him onto his back so that he could assess the damage inflicted. A nasty graze had emerged on the side of his bronzed cheek where his face had scraped across the ground while his headdress had become detached and fallen slightly so that it covered his eyes. Shaking her limbs back into life, Brightness joined her brother at Flint-Knife's side, listening to her injured team-mate's rasping breath.

Every gasp of air he took in seemed to cause him excruciating pain.

"Have strength friend," Sunfire whispered to him. "The gods will not want you dead yet."

Brightness knelt beside Flint-Knife, observing his wounded torso that was already showing signs of swelling and colouring of the skin. Gently, she lifted his headdress up so that the young man could see, noticing his eyes widen as he took quick breaths to try and fill his lungs.

"Slowly," she told him. "Slowly," and he nodded.

Brightness turned to looked up at her father who sat in his position above the court. He looked back at her for a moment before giving the briefest of signals to the High-Priest, who stood at his side. The High-Priest was an important part of the kingdom and had served Brightness's father for as long as she could remember. Only he and a few of his selected assistants were permitted to practice medicine. Not many things in life scared Brightness but the High-Priest was one of them. To begin with, he was unusually tall, towering over most of the men and women in the city, his large black-feathered headdress only adding to his height. Around his neck, a large beaded necklace clung to his heavily patterned skin, while holes in his teeth had been filled with jade gems. However, it was his eyes that unnerved Brightness the most. They were dark and lifeless, betraying no kind of emotion. When she was a very young child, Brightness had been bitten on the arm by a snake. It had sunk its gleaming fangs into her flesh and refused to release its grip. As Sunfire had battled to free her, she'd found herself staring at its eyes. They were cold and unblinking. Now, whenever she found herself in the High-Priest's company, that snake was the first thing that sprang into her mind.

Following the King's signal, the High-Priest descended the steps slowly before eventually arriving at Brightness's side. Crouching beside the stricken player, he pushed a small bottle to his lips and wiped his forehead with a damp cloth, before applying a thick green paste to his injured torso, his large fingers rubbing it into the skin. Seemingly oblivious to Flint-Knife's groans of pain, he continued his work, massaging the paste around the affected area and chanting softly. Brightness listened to his words, as he called upon the spirits to show mercy on the wounded player and forgive him for any mistakes that he had made in the way he had led his life. Sickness or injury would rarely ever be considered an accident; it would either be thought of as a punishment from the gods or that an evil spirit had captured your soul. Brightness couldn't imagine that such a brave and loyal young man as Flint-Knife could possibly have offended the gods in any way but it wasn't her place to ask such questions. Instead, she watched as the High-Priest continued his massage and prayer before finally, he lifted Flint-Knife to his feet and raised the young man's weary hand in the air as if to show the crowd that the game was ready to continue. They in turn roared their approval.

Brightness watched her team-mates' laboured movement as he staggered his way back into position, the colour drained from his cheeks. Pleadingly, she looked up at her father but he was unmoved. This didn't surprise her. The game was being held as an offering to the gods and needed to reach its conclusion. With war on the horizon, it would be foolish for her father to dishonour them in any way. Still, the sight of Flint-Knife in such clear discomfort troubled her. She stood at the back of the court as he picked up the ball and walked in her direction. He handed it to her but as he did so, his knees buckled and he fell forwards, only prevented from falling to the ground when she caught him in her arms. She held him for a moment before she let go, not knowing if he'd be able to stand on his own two feet.

"We must raise the hands of the victors," she said, nodding at the opposite side of the court. You should not suffer any longer."

She watched Flint-Knife's handsome face curl into a grimace. "The gods will not frown upon us," she said quietly. "They have already seen your courage."

Through gritted teeth, he managed to squeeze out a response. "In the days to come we will need the gods to bring us glory Brightness," he said. "I will not heap shame upon our great city by leaving the game before the Sun has fallen. We will play."

Her face flushed with defiance, she stood her ground, wrestling with the thoughts that swept through her mind. For a moment, she thought of throwing the ball into the baying crowd and walking off the court but before she could take such an action, Flint-Knife took the ball back from her, swivelled, and struck the ball with his forearm. It soared into the air and into the opposite side of the court, where Sunfire waited. Flicking out a hip, he returned the ball in Flint-Knife's direction, watching, along with everyone else at the ball court, to see how his opponent would react. Gingerly, Flint-Knife shuffled sideways, failing to suppress the gasps of pain that escaped from his mouth. He reached the ball with barely a moment to spare, groaning as he tried to strike it with a padded kneecap and sinking feebly to his knees as he saw the ball trickling pitifully along the floor to the side of the court. The point was lost and so Brightness thought to herself, was the game

And so, it proved to be. Although Flint-Knife somehow managed to continue, he was little more than a second body alongside Brightness, unable to manoeuvre his body into the ideal position to receive or return the ball. As the sun began to fall, and mercifully, the game began to reach its conclusion, Sunfire and his partner began to build an unassailable lead. There was only one possible way that Brightness could rescue a victory from the jaws of defeat. With time beginning to run out and knowing that there was no way to win on points, she began to take shots at the stone hoop whenever the opportunity arose, feeling a prickle of anger when the crowd began to mock her vain attempts to secure an unlikely victory. Darkness was now almost upon them and there was time for just one final play.

Standing on feet that were scratched and scorched, Brightness readied herself to receive her brother's serve. Struck with venom, it arrived in a blur of colour, leaving her little time to force her body into a reaction. Desperately, she managed to block it back into play, watching as Sunfire swept forward with an outstretched forearm, his dark eyes focused on the ball as he struck it with all his might. Defying the pain that engulfed his rib-cage, Flint-Knife somehow managed to flick the ball into the air, ready for Brightness to attack. Her lungs gasping for air, she burst forwards, and bending her legs and leaping into the air, she hit the ball with her right knee, sending it racing in the direction of the stone hoop above her. Heart thumping, she watched as it landed with a thud, seeing her strike near its target. For a moment, time slowed down and Brightness felt herself watching not only the ball, but the sea of faces at the court side, their facial reactions unfolding in slow-motion, mouths agape and eyes widening with shock as they recognised the accuracy of the shot. It couldn't possibly make it through the hoop, could it? Brightness felt her breath stick in her throat as the ball thudded into the jaws of the ring, rattling back and forth a few times before bouncing back out. Sorrowfully, it fell to the ground. The game was over and although Brightness had lost, she hoped that the gods would see that they had played with courage. Wearily, she embraced Sunfire and congratulated him on his victory before standing at the foot of the steps at the far end of the court. Forty steps above her, stood the temple. The High-Priest had taken his place within it. Hearing rasping breath behind her, she turned sharply to see that Flint-Knife had taken his place beside her. Exhausted though they both were, one final ordeal awaited them.

Chapter Three

The Gift Of Blood

Agonisingly slowly, they climbed towards the
temple. Every step that Flint-Knife took seemed to
send a shock through his injured body and Brightness
would notice his face crumple with pain. She had to
ignore the impulse to reach out and support him. He
had performed with great courage and could not allow
himself to display any sign of weakness now. The
ball game had always been an important way to bring
honour to the gods and the greater the bravery that
a player displayed, the more good fortune their city
would be receive – the gift of a plentiful crop harvest
or protection during times of war. Almost since the day
she had learned to walk, Brightness had realised that
the ball game had always been of great importance to
the people of her city. She'd listened to her father tell
her the spiritual story of the maize gods and the hero
twins so many times that she'd soon been able to recite
it word for word.

As the tale went, the Maize gods were keen ball
players who had been killed by the Lords of the
underworld for bothering them with their noisy game.
The head of one of the Maize gods was hung from a
tree within the underworld but as a daughter of the
Lords passed by, it spat into the palm of her hand,
magically impregnating her. This daughter bore two
sons who avenged their father and uncle's deaths
by finding their old ball and pads and becoming the

greatest and noisiest players that the Mayan kingdom had ever seen. This caused great anger to the Lords of the underworld who set about the task of killing the twins by setting them a series of deadly tests. Many times, they cheated death by using their great cunning, including escaping a house of flashing razor blades and a house full of ravenous jaguars. However, finally, they lost their lives, trapped in burning ovens. No-one could ever beat the Lords of death.

The ashes of the twins were scattered in a nearby river but the water had magical, life-giving powers. The twins were resurrected and with greater powers than ever before. They could cut any object up, including themselves, before returning it to its original state. For example, they could burn down a house and then recreate it moments later. Performing these feats of magic, they travelled from town to town until everyone in the land heard of their incredible act. Eventually, the Lords of death sent them an invitation to visit the underworld, unaware that they were the very twins they had once killed. The Lords were soon dazzled by the twins' magical performance and eager to join in with the festivities.

"Can you let me join in?" cried one Lord. "You may chop me up and then put me back together again?"

The twins obliged, only they did not fulfil their promise to put the Lord back together again afterwards. The other Lords knew that they had been defeated and allowed the twins to go back to the Earth's surface. Soon after their return, the gods of the heavens chose to honour the courage of the hero twins by bringing them up to the skies. One twin became the Sun and the other the moon. Their children were made the guardians of the Earth and from that day on they honoured their fathers by giving them the most precious possible gift. Ball courts were to be built in every town in the land and when every game was played, the people on Earth and the gods of the sky would remember their bravery.

Brightness and Flint-Knife were now no more than ten steps from reaching the High-Priest and the temple he stood within. As they approached, he stretched his arms out high above his head, making him even taller and more imposing than usual. Both fists clenched tightly, he addressed the crowd, who grew louder and more frenzied with each step that Brightness took.

"People of our great kingdom," the High-Priest roared, the black feathers of his headdress fluttering in the breeze. "I welcome your princess to the temple. May the gods of the sky smile upon her."

The crowd grew ever more animated as Brightness and Flint-Knife finally reached the temple and stood before the High-Priest. From this high vantage point, even in the fading light, she could see the thick jungle that stretched out beyond the walls of the city. In the periods when the crowd quietened, she could hear the intermittent calls of the howler monkeys rising above the constant buzz of the vast number of insects.

"We are a people of great power," the High-Priest continued, striking his heavily inked chest with one of his clenched fists. "A people of great strength. The gods of the sky have seen this and they will reward the courage that we have shown. With their guidance, we will fight our enemies until their bones are shattered and their flesh is torn. If they will it, they'll grant a great victory against the unspeakable evil that we face."

He stopped talking for a moment, stretching his arms wide once more, pacing from corner to corner of the temple and soaking in the crowd's feverish hollering.

"Oh mighty Itzamn," he shouted, tilting his head back so that his eyes looked skywards, "Lord of the heavens, master of night and day, we offer you this gift as a sign of our devotion to you, as a sign of our love for you, and to show you we are prepared to shed our people's blood in honour of your name."

Her heart drumming a furious rhythm, Brightness couldn't help fixing her eyes upon the stone altar that lay in the centre of the temple. Not many things frightened her in life. Not broken bones, not ripped flesh, not the creatures of the jungle. She would gladly give her life in battle if it would help defend her city but sadly, she knew her father would never agree to this. As he'd told her many times, she was too precious a jewel to lose. Now as the High-Priest towered above her, she couldn't stop the fear that gnawed at her heart. Before her grandfather's rule, when he put a stop to such evil, the temple she now stood in had been used to offer a human sacrifice from the losing players of the ball game. This would show their devotion to the gods. When they were very little, Sunfire had used to scare her by telling her of the blood that used to stream down the very steps she'd just climbed after a priest had driven a knife into the torso of a poor soul who lay upon the stone altar. Whenever she played on the ball court, the sight of the temple above her sent a chill through her veins.

Even though she knew that in these times, neither she nor Flint-Knife would lose their lives, Brightness felt the palms of her hands grow clammy and her throat grow ever drier. She studied the High-Priest's dead eyes as he took Flint-Knife by the arm and motioned to the young man that he should lie on the altar. He took an unsteady pace forward before finding his path blocked. Brightness now stood between him and the altar.

"It would please the gods to send them royal blood," she cried. "It would be an honour."

For once, the High-Priest seemed unsure of himself. He turned and looked down at his King, with Brightness also scanning her father's face for signs of a reaction. There followed an agonising wait, the crowd falling deathly silent until finally the King, sitting stone-faced beside his queen, gave the faintest of nods.

Trying to control her rapid breathing, Brightness allowed the High-Priest to lead her to the stone altar. Rather than lie back upon it, she turned and knelt before it so that she faced the crowd. Standing beside her, the High-Priest held his brightly coloured staff, lifting it up towards the heavens and beginning to shout once more.

"Lord of the heavens," he repeated, "we offer you this royal blood, as a sign of our devotion. May you honour us with a great victory when the time comes."

Reaching a hand up to his headdress, he pulled out a small, knotted piece of rope, no longer than half the size of Brightness's forearm. However, buried within it, lay a collection of sharp thorns, the sight of which made her heart race ever faster. She steeled herself as the High-Priest handed her the knotted rope before unfolding a roll of bark cloth that he held within his hands. She knew what she must do but couldn't help hesitating at the thought of it. She looked down at the sea of faces watching her every move from below and felt a lump form in her throat, eventually turning her head to the side and facing the High-Priest.

"Are you afraid Princess?" he said softly, locking his dark eyes into hers. "The gods will not smile upon those who show cowardice."

A flicker of anger rising in her chest, Brightness lifted the knotted rope to her mouth. Returning the High-Priest's stare as he held the bark cloth beneath her chin, she dragged it slowly across her tongue, the sharp thorns drawing her blood. The pain was excruciating, with her mouth feeling like it had been set alight, but she was determined not to show it. A faint trace of a smile formed on the High-Priest's face as he allowed the blood to drip onto the bark cloth.

"Once more Princess," he said. "Once more and the gods will be satisfied."

Summoning all the strength that she could muster, Brightness did as she was told, feeling the warmth of her sticky blood dripping through the piercings formed by the thorns. Her ordeal over, she rose unsteadily to her feet, trying her best to blink away the tears forming in her eyes and watching the High-Priest go about his work. Carrying the blood-filled tree bark, he placed it within a clay bowl that he had placed upon the altar, before setting fire to the dry leaves that lay at its base. As the flames flickered gently, Brightness watched a thin trail of smoke rise into the air. Her blood would now be received by Itzamn. She hoped that the Lord of the heavens would reward her city for the sacrifice.

Chapter Four

Surging Fear

To Brightness, the jungle seemed quieter today, almost as if the creatures that dwelt there were aware of the army of men that would soon arrive with their axes and spears. Since she and Sunfire had been small children, they had listened to her father tell her that she must never be afraid. The speech he'd made to his people the previous day, she'd heard on more occasions than she could remember. Show the gods your courage, he would tell them, and they will reward you. Only the boldest can succeed in this life. Brightness had tried her utmost to heed her father's words, demanding that she should be allowed to learn to fight alongside the fiercest warriors in the kingdom, learning fast, until she could stand her ground with just about anyone, including her brother. Of course, to her father's pride, both of his children had also displayed great prowess on the ball court, playing the game with determination, resilience and skill.

However, as much as Brightness had tried to dismiss fear from her heart, today it surged through her veins like a deadly infection. War would soon be waged upon their city and as much as her father talked of trusting in the gods to guide them, she could only think of the size of the army on their way to overwhelm them. Her uncle, Dark Eyes, who ruled over the great city of Tikal, had declared war on his own brother. Years earlier, he and her father had fought side by side for many years to overthrow their enemies and seize power themselves. It had been agreed that her uncle, who had always been the most ambitious of the two, would rule over the kingdom they had overthrown, while her father was rewarded by being given the smaller outpost of Dos Pilas, about four days' march away. For many years, this division of wealth had proved to be ideal for all parties, with her uncle enjoying the great power he now wielded and her father building a prosperous splinter-state of his own, with fertile lands and widespread trade routes. Sadly, over time, Brightness had witnessed the deterioration of her father's relationship with his brother. On the few occasions in which they had visited Tikal, she'd never warmed to her uncle, finding him to be cold in his manner and unnecessarily cruel to those who he believed opposed him. She could see that it brought great sadness to her father when they disagreed on any matters of state, with her uncle becoming ever more unreasonable in his demands over land and taxes. When he eventually refused to cave in anymore, her uncle had treated this as an act of treason. Now his army of men made their way through the jungle, ready to burn Dos Pilas to the ground.

With only two, possibly three sunsets left before her uncle's threatened invasion Brightness's father had taken his two children hunting.

"The defence of the city is prepared," he'd told them when they'd looked at him through anxious eyes, "and my fate is now in the hands of the gods. If it is their will, then soon I will die and I will not spend my final days cowering behind my walls. I will spend them in the beauty of these forests with my children."

In the stillness, they moved with light feet until they came to the water hole. It had always been their father's favourite place to hunt. There they sat for some time, not speaking but just taking in the beauty of the mossy-green water as it fell from the rocks above and collected in a circular pool. So thick were the trees that towered above them, that only thin streaks of light snaked their way through, lighting up small sections of the water. On the opposite side of the water, lay a treacherous path that led up to the head of the waterfall, the passage of time leaving the rock broken and unstable in places. When they were feeling adventurous, she and Sunfire enjoyed climbing up to the cavern that hid behind the rushing water, sitting behind the falls and tossing rocks into the still water below.

It was a while before they caught sight of the peccary on the opposite side of the pool, leaning its short snout into the water. Sunfire noticed it first, raising his hand slowly and signalling with his eyes. They were on their feet in a flash, moving steadily but purposefully into the cover of the trees. Closer to the animal, they crept in silence, eventually slithering along on their bellies as they moved within range of their prey. Brightness, who had moved to the front of the three, reached a hand down to her belt and withdrew the long, thin tube that hung from her waist. Propping herself up on her elbows, she placed a dart laced with frog poison within it before lifting the weapon to her mouth. Wincing a little due to the pain in her wounded tongue, she steadied herself and took aim but just as she was ready to release the dart, the peccary turned away from the water and caught sight of her. Surprisingly, it didn't react and run immediately but remained remarkably still, either not recognising the danger it was in or perhaps too frightened to react decisively. Brightness too, was caught off guard and found herself locking eyes with the creature as it stared back at her. For a moment, neither of them flinched, with an eerie silence hanging in the air. Even the cicadas seemed to have ceased their constant chirping and only the gentle sound of the water falling into the pool could be heard. Finally, after it seemed an age had passed, the animal burst into life, leaping to its left and heading for the safety of the surrounding bushes. Brightness reacted within a heartbeat, drawing in a deep breath before exhaling sharply and propelling the poisoned dart towards her target. It struck the peccary in its side, piercing the flesh that clung to its rib cage, causing it to let out a high-pitched squeal as it thundered into the undergrowth. Brightness made no attempt to run after the animal, knowing it wouldn't get far with the venom beginning to work its way into its bloodstream and paralysing its muscles. Along with her father and brother, she followed its tracks through the forest before finding its lifeless body lying in a small clearing.

Fashioning a fire, Sunfire and Blazing Sky feasted on the meat from the peccary and ate until their stomachs ached. It was with some bitterness that Brightness watched them devour their food, her injured tongue making the chewing of tough meat an impossibility.

"Not hungry little sister," Sunfire teased, noticing the scowl etched on her face and smiling at the anger that flashed in her eyes. As much as he loved her, from time to time, he enjoyed provoking his fiery sibling. He took another piece of meat and made a point of showing Brightness how delicious it tasted, licking his lips and leaning back against the tree he sat against and stretching his legs out in front of him, smiling at the scowl he received in return.

In silence, Brightness waited for them to finish eating. She knew that her father had brought them out here to talk and she was eager to hear what he had to say.

"My children," he said eventually, "it is time for me to speak my mind. As you know, the city that we love faces the gravest of threats and soon the gods will pass judgement on me. My brother has allowed jealousy and bitterness to cloud his mind but I will not allow him to destroy what our family has built. Not while the blood still flows through my veins and I have strength left in my body. My warriors may be fewer in number but they are fierce in spirit. They are prepared to fight for our city with axes in their hands and pride in their hearts."

"It will be an honour to fight alongside you Father," Sunfire began, "A great victory will be ours."

Standing as tall as she could, Brightness grasped her brother's hand. "I will fight too," she managed to mumble, her tongue throbbing.

Blazing Sky smiled at his children's courage.

"My children," he said. "I have been blessed by the Lords of the skies when you were brought into this world. I would be proud to have you fight by my side but you are still young and this war is not yours to fight. If the gods decide that my life has drawn to an end and my brother stands victorious, then negotiations will begin to arrange the price our city must pay for this war. If I am to fail, then there is no reason why you should die too."

"But Father," Sunfire said, when Blazing Sky had fallen silent for a moment, "if the walls to our city are breached then I cannot stand by and watch. I will fight until our enemy is defeated or I lie in the dirt."

"You will not have to my son," Blazing Sky replied. This war need only provide one death before it is ended. My brother understands that too."

Chapter Five

Just One Death

It was just after sunrise when Brightness saw the first of her uncle's warriors emerge from the cover of the trees. Standing high upon the walls that protected their small city, she touched her father's arm gently.

"I see him," Blazing Sky responded as the warrior held his ground, some way in the distance, wary of the threat of arrows that could whistle towards him at any moment. There he stayed for a moment with the bright orange feathers from his headdress gleaming in the morning sunlight. His skin was covered from head to toe in small black dots in honour of the jaguar, fierce predator of the jungle, while in his right hand he held a long spear which stood almost as tall as he was. His opposite fist clenched a circular shaped shield with an elaborate green and gold pattern snaking its way through the centre. For a while, this lone warrior waited, almost daring an attack on him to be made before finally a second figure arrived to stand at his side. Before long, a whole stream of fierce looking men were stretched out in the clearing, all armed and ready to fight.

Her stomach churning, Brightness watched her father's archers who lined the defensive walls. They began to lift their weapons, only stopping when he raised his hand and held it in position. Still, the warriors streamed through from the forest, each as ferocious looking as the next. Eventually, sitting astride a tall platform, supported by four strong, bare chested men, Brightness caught sight of her uncle. A fearsome sight, steadily he approached the walls of the city, a shiny golden serpent sitting at the base of his headdress, the two sharp fangs sliding their way down to his cheekbones. Streaks of red and white dye stretched out across his muscular torso, a necklace of assorted gemstones hanging from his thick neck. Studying his cruel face, Brightness found it difficult to believe that the same blood flowed through his and her father's veins.

It seemed to take an eternity for her uncle to creep ever closer to the city walls. With every measured step that the platform carriers took, Brightness felt her heart grow heavier inside her chest until finally, no more than a good spear throw away, they stopped. Her forehead beginning to perspire, she looked on as her uncle climbed down from his platform, standing tall and fearless before his enemies.

"Proud people of Dos Pilas," he shouted, "My name is Dark Eyes and I present my army in front of you today. If I command it, they will send burning arrows to set alight your city, they will scale your walls and cut down your men, women and children. Your blood will soak the earth upon which you live and the creatures of the forest will pick at your dead flesh and bones in the days that follow." He paused, leaving his words hanging in the air for a moment. "If it is the will of the gods for your city to perish, then so be it," he continued gravely, "but I believe that the spilling of blood can be avoided." Pointing his finger upwards at Blazing Sky, he raised his voice to an even greater volume.

"For years, I have allowed my love for my brother and his family to cloud my senses. Many times, I held my tongue as his actions insulted the kingdom of Tikal, telling myself that a great ruler must show loyalty to those who share their blood, but I cannot allow myself to show weakness any longer or the gods will pass judgement on my cowardice. I must act quickly and without mercy before I dishonour my people."

Stretching out his long arms and glancing towards the heavens, he fell silent again briefly before returning his gaze to meet that of Blazing Sky who stood unmoved high upon the city walls. Brightness stole a look at her father's face, noting that his expression had not changed a bit. There was no fear, no anger, just a proud man at peace with himself. She marvelled at how calm he managed to stay, since her own heart seemed to pound ever faster with every word that left her uncle's mouth.

"Brave warriors of Dos Pilas, the Lords of the skies have spoken to me," her uncle continued once more. "They will accept one death rather than see the slaughter of many. My brother cannot be allowed to continue to walk upon this earth but I will leave your city standing if you give him to me and open your gates in peace. Who will make this sacrifice for their family?"

He looked directly up at Blazing Sky. "What do you say brother? How loyal are your people? Mine would give their lives for me. We'll soon find out if yours will too."

Her throat growing ever drier, Brightness looked at the archers to either side of her, then down at the warriors collected in the courtyard below. It would only take one arrow or one spear to the back to end her father's life. It could save their family, it could save their city, Even the most loyal of her father's men wouldn't be able to resist such a thought from entering their minds. The wait was agonising but not one man moved a muscle, A mixture of relief and pride rising inside her chest, Brightness glared down defiantly at Dark Eyes. Now he could see for himself the love and loyalty her father inspired. Even from a distance, she was sure she could see her uncle's eyes narrowing with anger. As much as he tried to hide it, he was agitated now. Brightness could hear it in his voice.

"Your people are foolish brother," he said, "and their blood will soon flow into the earth. I will grant you a final chance to save them. Brother, show your love for those who live within your city walls by throwing yourself from where you stand. The Lords of the skies will be satisfied with one death. You have my word that your family and your people will be spared."

Brightness held her breath as her father took one step higher so that he stood tall upon the walls of the city. She was grateful that the air was hot and still today, for the slightest breeze against her father's back could send him plummeting to the ground below. When he eventually spoke, not a sound could be heard.

"My brother," he said calmly, his facial expression never changing, "your mind has become poisoned with bitterness, greed and jealousy. This has torn away at my heart for many years now and caused me great sorrow. You rule your kingdom through fear and cruelty and bring dishonour to our family. When you stand before so many and speak false words, the gods will see you for what you truly are – a liar who is no longer fit to lead your people. You say the Lords of the skies will accept one death on this day. I say that we should let them decide whose blood that they seek. In front of your people and my own, I propose that we fight in single combat. No other man, woman or child need throw a spear or swing an axe. The cities that we helped create can continue to thrive rather than lie in ruins. Once again brother, I ask you to dismiss any cowardice from your heart and to stand before your people and fight. Let them see that a true warrior leads them. If you defeat me then I grant you the keys to my city and whatever rewards that you deem yours to take. Before the gods, you have my word that my people will not oppose you and offer resistance. In return, if I am to be the victor, then your army should turn on its heel and leave our land, never to return. This vow you must make."

Brightness watched her uncle as he turned to one of his aides who stood at his side, an animated conversation taking place between the two of them. It was impossible for anyone to know what was being said and Brightness felt her heart begin to pound once more. Skilled warrior that her father was, she knew that her uncle too, was renowned for his fearsome strength on the battlefield. Her father had often spoken proudly of his brother's daring deeds before their relationship had soured, telling her stories of him cutting down row upon row of enemies as they'd seized power all those years ago. The golden serpent on his head gleaming, she watched her uncle turn his attention to her father once more.

"Brother, we may now be enemies but I cannot deny the truth in what you propose. There need be no further blood shed than our own today. The Lords of the skies will see that I will show people mercy. No man or woman shall be cut down where they stand and I will only take from you what I am rightfully owed. I deliver this vow to you. When the sun rises tomorrow, we will settle our quarrel. May the gods decide who should die."

Chapter Six

The Time For Talk Is Over

Her eyes growing tired and raw, Brightness stood behind her father as he sat on a small wooden chair that lay at the far wall of his sleeping chambers. She hadn't managed to sleep at all during the night, for when she closed her eyes, she found herself unable to escape the image of her uncle's fierce face, running towards the city walls, eyes ablaze with anger, his war club raised high and ready to strike. Outside, the city was still smothered in darkness but it wouldn't be long before the first rays of sunlight emerged. Brightness had always thought that there was no finer sight than the sun rising above the lush forests and the world beginning to burst into life. This morning though, she would take no joy in such things, longing for the skies to remain black for as long as possible.

Gently, she tied his orange pati around his neck so that it hung across his shoulders before lifting his headdress into position, the hooked beak of the owl's face hovering just above his nose, its gleaming yellow eyes bright and brilliant.

"Are you sure you must do this, Father?" Sunfire asked from the other side of the room. "Our warriors are strong and would follow you straight to the underworld if you commanded it. They are ready to fight for you, Father. This is not your war alone."

He rose to his feet, crossed the room and took Blazing Sky's hands within his.

"I am ready to fight for you too father," he said quietly.

Blazing Sky closed his eyes briefly.

"I didn't start this war," he said calmly, "but today, live or die, I will bring it to an end. I will ask no man to risk his life for me, not even my son. We will let the gods decide if I am to triumph."

Sunfire started to protest but he stopped himself before the words escaped from his mouth. He knew from experience that once his father had made up his mind, it was pointless arguing with him. Silently, he picked up his father's macuahuitl and placed it within his right hand. The weapon was a mixture of beauty and horror. Carved lovingly from the finest of wood, the face of a jaguar had been etched into the flattened top of the club, its eyes a burning orange, Below it, lay an intricately designed pattern with an image of the sun at its centre. However, as much as you could find yourself admiring the skill and care that had been put into forging such an item, there was also no escaping the fact that it was an instrument of death. Lining the sides of the wood, were rows of razor-sharp blades and when swung in anger, this deadly club could inflict terrible damage on flesh and bone.

Trying to force thoughts of her father and her uncle wielding such savage weapons, Brightness walked to the far side of the chambers and retrieved the shield that rested against the wall. Circular in shape and with the proud face of an owl matching her father's headdress, she strapped it over his forearm. The previous evening, she and her mother had worked for hours, to create the picture, working long after darkness had fallen to apply the coloured dyes to the animal hide, before attaching it to the thick bamboo cane that formed the strong underlayer. Ever since she was a little girl, Brightness's mother had taught her how to create murals that would cover the walls of their home, carve wood to make sculptures and decorate pottery with elaborate designs. Along with the playing of the ball game, she could think of no better way to occupy her days.

"If the gods choose not to protect you, then this might," she said quietly, her power of speech only slowly returning.

Her father smiled before wrapping his bronzed arms around her. Their entire past was in the embrace – hunting in the forests, teaching her the rules of the ball game, learning how to fight like a warrior should.

"My spirit rests within this shield," Brightness told him, "When it is in your hands, then I will be with you."

There was nothing more to say and with the first rays of morning sunlight flickering outside, there was little time left. Blazing Sky stood up tall and proud, not a sign of fear on his face as Brightness and Sunfire stood on either side of him, each taking his arm in theirs. Together they walked the short distance to the gates of their city where their mother and the High-Priest waited. High up above them, lining the walls of the city were rows of her father's warriors, all grave of face and sombre in mood. When the three of them reached the gates, Blazing Sky released his arms from his children's grip and embraced their mother warmly, whispering something inaudible into her ear and wiping a tear gently from her cheek. Brightness felt her legs weaken as she watched him accompany the High-Priest towards the entrance, flinching a little as the huge gates began to creak open to reveal the huge army of men standing before the forest. Some distance in front of them, she saw her uncle waiting.

Feeling her mother tugging at her arm, she turned. They were expected to take their places in the seats just below the temple alongside other various dignitaries of the city. From this vantage point, they would have a perfect view of the 'event'.

Brightness took her seat, a tight knot forming in her stomach. Below her, as many people as possible had crammed onto the temple's steps. Perched up high above them, almost as if she was on display, she felt a sudden prickle of self-consciousness. She saw some people point up at her and stare and it made her feel even more anxious than she already was, finding herself gripping hold of Sunfire's hand as he sat beside her. She hadn't held his hand since they were small children and she was ashamed to find hers shaking.

"A princess should show more courage," she thought to herself. This is the time to show your strength."

Composing herself, she looked down below the city walls and saw her father striding out across the ground, the High-Priest at his side, until they were almost face to face with her uncle. She couldn't help gasping as they stood opposite each other. Her father, not a small man himself, looked almost child-like in comparison to his brother whose huge body looked as if it had been sculpted from stone.

"Don't worry little sister," she heard Sunfire whisper. "No man that size can move with speed. Father won't fight him up close. He will tire him out and then cut him down."

Brightness found herself nodding in agreement but her heart weighed ever heavier within her chest.

Blazing Sky was now no more than three spear

lengths away from his brother, close enough to see the bitterness painted across his face.

"I thought you might stay hidden behind your walls brother," Dark Eyes greeted him fiercely. "It may have been better for you if you had done so but I congratulate you on your boldness."

"It is not too late brother. You can turn your army around and march back to Tikal. Join me within the walls of my city as my guest and let us see if we can announce peace between our two great kingdoms. Blood need not be spilt today."

Blazing Sky studied his brother's face and for a fleeting moment thought he saw the faintest sign of regret in his eyes.

"My men have travelled too far," Dark Eyes said, "and I cannot show weakness before them. Your disloyalty has caused me great pain brother. When the skies grow dark tonight, I will mourn your death and think of the times when we were allies, but die you must. The gods demand it." He turned an outstretched arm towards the army that stood behind him. "Look at my warriors brother. Look at how they stand ready to fight for me – their king. There is no kingdom that they will not take for me."

"Am I meant to tremble before them?" Blazing Sky responded. "It brings me sorrow to see thousands march for one man's greed. I can see that the time for talk is over. When you lie in the dust and I stand above you I will try and remember a time when I could think of you as my brother and not my enemy."

The High-Priest stepped forward between the two of them.

"It is the will of the Lords of the skies that these men will fight to the death," he announced. "May the blood that is offered today bring our kingdoms great wealth and glory. May those who dwell in the heavens grant us rain to let our crops grow and from this day onwards let our cities form an alliance that cannot be broken. The gods have spoken to me and recognise these men have chosen to settle this war in single combat. They demand that no man or woman should seek revenge if their king should fall and should honour the agreement that has been made. Those who attempt to do so will be struck down with sickness and disease for the rest of their days, until the skin drops from their bones and they make their journey to the underworld."

From high up on the temple steps, Brightness watched as the High-Priest stepped back towards her father, helping remove the pati from his shoulders and holding a small bottle to his lips. Inside it, would be a frothy liquid made from crushed cocoa beans, chilli peppers and water. Her father, along with many others in the city, believed this 'xocolatl' was the drink of the gods themselves and brought him great strength and wisdom. He often drank it before they went hunting or during religious ceremonies. Such was his belief in this drink, he'd even asked Brightness and her mother to paint a mural of him enjoying it on the walls of the city temple. Brightness found it a little bitter herself, and certainly hadn't felt her speed or strength increasing when trying it, but she hoped it would help her father now. With her uncle's towering figure approaching with his war club in hand, he'd need all the assistance he could get.

Chapter Seven

The Gods Make Their Choice

Rigid in her seat, Brightness held her breath as Dark Eyes charged forward, taking a huge swing in the direction of her father's head. She saw the sharp blades gleam in the sunlight and had to force herself to keep her eyes open. Mercifully, Blazing Sky was quick on his feet, spinning away as the club hurtled towards him. Again, like a raging bull, her uncle attacked but this time found her father's shield, thudding into the face of the owl that she had painted for him and tearing a jagged line through its middle. The crowds of people on the steps below let out a collective gasp of air as the power of the blow sent their king stumbling backwards momentarily, only recovering just in time to duck beneath Dark's Eyes club as it whistled through the air.

Although there was little finesse to her uncle's fighting style, Brightness could see how his sheer size and savagery had overwhelmed previous foes and despite his bulk he moved with deceptive speed. She felt completely helpless and frustrated knowing that there was nothing she could do to help her father.

The pattern continued, with Dark Eyes the aggressor, swinging his war club in a barrage of furious blows, each seemingly more murderous than the last with Blazing Sky's agility only just helping him avoid having his head removed from his shoulders. Ducking beneath the blades of his opponent's weapon or sidestepping at the very last moment, he managed to nullify any attacks but how long could he continue to do so? Brightness found herself grinding her teeth and flinching every time club thudded into shield. Finally, her father managed a counterattack of his own, gracefully leaning back out of striking range before springing forward with his own club and landing a glancing blow against Dark's Eyes left shoulder, the blades tearing into his skin. The crowds below Brightness roared out in joy and she too found herself forgetting any thoughts of noble restraint and leaping to her feet. The wound itself was nothing too serious but it seemed to have a huge effect on both men. All of a sudden, Blazing Sky began to swarm all over his brother, the larger man now visibly more ponderous, as if left in shock by the realisation his flesh could be pierced. Feinting low before springing high, flicking away with his club deftly, Brightness watched her father take control of the battle, his weapon once again striking Dark Eyes, this time on his left hip. Again, it was only a faint contact but enough to allow a trickle of blood to seep through his clothing.

Erupting with furious rage, Dark Eyes attacked with an even greater fury but so wild were his swings that it wasn't difficult for Blazing Sky to evade his clumsy advances. So nimble was his footwork that he made his opponent stumble after one looping attack had failed to find its target, raising a few faint chuckles from the steps of the temple. They died out quickly but there was doubting that the tide of the battle had turned. Dark Eyes may as well have been trying to hack away at a fly, his anger growing with every miss. "He is tiring too," Brightness thought to herself, "Just as Sunfire said he would." She gripped her brother's hand, the other balled into a clenched fist, so tightly held that her knuckles had turned a ghostly white.

Summoning every fragment of strength that remained within his body, Dark Eyes came forward once more, club raised towards the heavens, breathing heavily from his exertions. The serpent of his headdress shining, he charged, a ferocious, whirling blaze of gold. Blazing Sky continued to fight with patience, parrying away blow after blow and waiting for an opening of his own. Finally, as his brother's club whistled over his head, a chance presented itself. Such was the force that Dark Eyes used to mount his latest attack, when he missed his target, he found himself off balance and vulnerable to a counter strike. In a flash, Blazing Sky swung his own club past his opponent's shield and towards his unguarded neck. Desperately attempting to defend himself, Dark Eyes reacted by bringing up his striking arm at the last moment, blocking what would have been a deadly blow by positioning the base of his own club in the path of the oncoming weapon. The mighty crack that followed the impact filled the air and there was a collective intake of breath from those who watched as Dark Eyes' club snapped in two. Both he and Blazing Sky seemed to stand still for a moment, frozen in place, as they watched the top half of the weapon hurtle skywards before landing with a thud upon the dust covered earth.

Brightness watched her uncle begin to stagger backwards, his eyes consumed with panic, the shattered handle of his club still resting pathetically in his grasp. For a moment the two men stared across at each other, each taking a while to register what had occurred. The temptation for her uncle to turn and flee must have been overwhelming Brightness thought to herself but he must know that he cannot. To be forever remembered as a coward would be a fate worse than death. If these were to be his last moments on Earth, he would not spend them fleeing in front of his people. Instead, he stood there in the dust, breathing heavily, no more than a light stone's throw away from his opponent. Her throat tightening, Brightness saw her father begin to step forward cautiously, his eyes never leaving his foe for a moment. Surprisingly, for one so light on his feet, his movements were now slow and laboured as if every step were an effort to make. Brightness twitched in her seat as she watched her father halt his advance and stand completely still, his whole body seeming to sway. She stole a glance at Sunfire, seeing the alarm on his face. Was their father injured? She hadn't seen him take a blow and there were no visible signs of a wound. To her horror, he looked completely exhausted, and although the battle had been fought with frenetic energy, the sudden change in him was shocking. She found herself on her feet, all thought of noble dignity forgotten, her legs buckling as she stood. Something was wrong. Below her she could see the concern painted on the watching faces of the crowd.

Blazing Sky, sweat streaming down his forehead and into his eyes, forced his weakening body forwards, but he hadn't taken more than three or four steps before his legs betrayed him and he fell to one knee. Brightness, her hands shaking, watched him return to his feet slowly. Something was wrong. Something was badly wrong. Without thinking, she began to descend the steps, only halted when Sunfire refused to release the grip he had on her hand, pulling her back towards him and wrapping her in his powerful arms. Below them, they saw their uncle pounce. Initially hesitant, he'd realised that Blazing Sky was either exhausted or suffering from a wound and sprang forward with an explosive fury. Throwing away his shield, with all his might, he ran at Blazing Sky, ducking under his brother's desperate swing of his club, and knocking him off his feet. Within the dust, they wrestled on the ground, almost as if locked in a curious embrace while all who watched tried to make sense of what they were seeing.

Brightness felt the blood surge through her veins as she looked on breathlessly. Neither man appeared to have gained the upper hand but it was difficult to tell with the pale yellow clouds that emerged with every swing of an arm or kick of a leg. Her father's club had been knocked from his grasp when he'd fallen while his shield too now lay on the floor, the eyes of the owl staring up into the skies. The wind, once so gentle, had picked up now, blowing Brightness's long hair in front of her face and further obscuring her vision. All she could do was wait and hope along with the thousands of silent faces who stood below her. Finally, a figure rose wearily to its feet, smothered so thickly with dust that it was difficult to make out its form.

"People of Dos Pilas," Brightness heard her uncle bellow. "Your king is dead. He fought with bravery but the gods have chosen me as their victor. Let there be no further ill will between us and honour my brother's word. My men will march through your gates unchallenged and I will meet with you to discuss the terms of your surrender."

Straining her tear-filled eyes, Brightness could just about make out the stricken body of her father, unable to look away. When she finally did so, she looked up to the skies, watching a lone eagle soaring way above the forests until finally it disappeared from view.

Chapter Eight

You Still Have Your Children

Still in a state of shock, Brightness stood at her mother's side within the great hall, Sunfire to their left and a few of her father's most trusted men nearby. Her mother, Brightness thought to herself, was a truly beautiful sight today, sat high upon the delicately chiselled throne, the colourful green feathers of her headdress matching the jade necklace she wore around her neck. She sat in silence, strong and proud, although a great sorrow lay within her dark eyes. There was no time to mourn. That would come later but now it was time to make peace with Dark Eyes. However much she hated to do so, she would have to for the sake of her people. He had by far the more powerful army and to defy him openly would probably result in the city being burnt to the ground and its people, including her own children, slaughtered. Besides, her husband had given his word to Dark Eyes that the victor of their battle would decide on the terms of the peace that followed. Even after his death, Blazing Sky's word meant something.

Brightness knew this too. Inside, her heart boiled with anger but she steeled herself to remain calm and respectful. Her uncle must not think of she or Sunfire as a threat to him. If he did, then he would not think twice about having them killed. She heard footsteps approaching and took a deep breath of air. Finding a stray tear rolling down her cheek, she wiped her eyes quickly before anyone saw. Not that she was sure

she wanted to, neither she, her mother or Sunfire had
even had time to see her father's body yet. The High-
Priest had seen that it was carried straight to the temple
where it lay in state. The burial would be arranged soon
enough but first they must deal with her uncle.

They didn't have long to wait, with the footsteps
growing ever louder until Dark Eyes appeared, flanked
by a number of his men on one side and the High-Priest
on the other. An uncomfortable time passed before, they
reached the throne.

"My Queen," the High-Priest said, "I stand before
you today with the heaviest of hearts. It was the will
of the gods that our great king has been taken from us
today and his time on this Earth has come to an end. He
left this world as he lived in it – a warrior and a man of
his word."

Brightness stole a glance at her mother's face,
studying it for a reaction. She remained impassive.

"My Queen," the High-Priest continued. "Dark Eyes,
King of Tikal, stands before you bearing no ill feeling.
Any quarrel between he and your husband has ended
and today marks a new beginning in the relationship
between our two great cities."

"Then let the King tell me so himself," Brightness
heard her mother say a little sharply.

Dark Eyes stepped forward in front of the High-
Priest, the golden serpent upon his head no longer
gleaming but covered in dust.

"Your priest speaks the truth," he said, "I have no
appetite to see the destruction of your city and the proud
people that live within it. My brother and I had reached
the point where no words could heal the wounds we'd
inflicted on each other. Now our differences have been
settled for good and we can look forward to our cities

being blessed with wealth and glory."

"And of what use is wealth and glory without your loved ones to share it?" asked the Queen icily, her face still expressionless.

Dark Eyes glowered angrily, only just maintaining his composure.

"You still have your children," he said menacingly. "Even in times of great loss, we must be grateful that our flesh and blood lives on."

He looked directly at Brightness and then at Sunfire.

"Unless the gods decide that they must be taken from us," he said.

For a moment noone spoke and now Brightness saw her mother's eyes soften for the first time.

"My husband was a man of his word," she said. "He gave his life for the people of Dos Pilas and would not want to see more children lose their fathers. I will put my sorrow to one side if it means we can agree to a peace between our two kingdoms."

Brightness saw her uncle's eyes narrow, his cruel face showing no warmth or compassion. "Today I will hold my tongue," she thought to herself, "but there will come a time when our people are strong enough to defeat your armies and I will enjoy watching you suffer as we have done."

"My Queen," the High-Priest began, breaking the silence, "The gods have blessed Dark Eyes with the strength to win a great battle. As our great king declared himself, his victory should allow him to claim whatever reward he deems fit."

"And what reward should the gods give a man who has slain his brother?" the Queen said.

Dark Eyes smiled. "A warrior like me can take

whatever he wishes," he said dismissively. "And kill whoever insults them."

The High-Priest intervened. "Dark Eyes demands that he fill ten chests with the gold, jade and pottery of his choice. These riches are just reward for the courage that he has displayed."

The Queen sat stone faced before giving a faint nod.

"The King also demands that Dos Pilas increases the taxes they pay to Tikal, sharing the wealth that they have gained from trade in food and goods with far greater generosity that they have in the past."

Brightness was amazed that her mother stayed restrained after this insult. Her uncle's greed was clear for all see. Whatever tax had been paid to him over the years was never enough. Always, he desired more.

Again, the Queen forced a slight nod of approval at the demands.

"Does it end now?" she asked. "Tikal and its king have been rewarded handsomely. There is little left for us to give. When the sun next rises, we will bury my husband. We will not seek to avenge his death and will respect the peace that has been settled on this day."

"Dark Eyes will march his men away from the gates of Dos Pilas once he is satisfied that no threat to Tikal is posed by your city."

"Dark Eyes has my word. I will be true to it – just as my husband was."

"Forgive me my Queen," the High Priest said, "for though Dark Eyes trusts your word, he cannot dismiss the possibility that another of your citizens will ignore your orders. That is why he must ask for something that will prevent any such unpleasantness."

Brightness was confused. What was her uncle asking

for? What more could they possibly surrender to him?

Dark Eyes strode forward so that he stood at the steps that led to the throne.

"I must take your son," he said. "He will live with me in Tikal, where I can keep him close. Already, he has grown strong. Strong enough to lead your warriors against me when the time is right. I will not allow this."

Speaking directly to Sunfire, he continued.

"You will not be harmed," he said. "You will be free to walk our city and enjoy all that is within our walls but you must not tread beyond them."

Brightness could hear her mother's voice crack a little when she responded.

"You are taking him as your prisoner," she said, "and if any of my people break our agreement then he will be killed."

"But as you have given me your word that your people will not seek to damage the terms of our peace, then this will never happen. I will treat Sunfire as if he was my own son," Dark Eyes said.

"But I have seen how you treat your own family Dark Eyes," she said sadly. "My son's place is by my side and I will never agree to give him up. My warriors will fight until the last of them is in the ground before Sunfire leaves for Tikal."

Dark Eyes' face become clouded with anger.

"What sort of queen would allow her city to burn in order to keep their son close to them?" he said. "You have until the sun falls to give Sunfire to me or I will not agree to peace between us."

With that, he motioned to his men and turned to leave, making it half-way towards the exit before a shout stopped him in his tracks.

"Uncle stop," Sunfire shouted. "I will accompany you to Tikal."

The whole hall was stunned into silence, Brightness and her mother both turning in disbelief.

"This is the right thing to do Mother," Sunfire continued, as she stared at him through widened eyes. "Leaving our great city will break my heart but I would rather live a life of sorrow than see all that my father built destroyed."

He turned back towards Dark Eyes. "When the sun next rises, we will bury him, and then I will march with you to Tikal."

"Even at his tender age, your son is wise," Dark Eyes told the Queen. He thinks not of himself but his people. Can you do the same?"

Seeing her shaking, Brightness reached out and placed the palm of her hand on top of her mother's. It seemed an age before she responded, eyes watering as she switched her gaze between Sunfire and Dark Eyes. Brightness felt her legs growing ever more unsteady, her head throbbing as the blood rushed through her skull. Her father's body was not yet cold and now she would lose her brother too.

"My son will go with you," she heard her mother say.

Chapter Nine

His Blood Is Not Yours To Give

The skies were still black when Brightness crept from her bed. Slinking her way through the shadows like a cat, she found herself at the bottom of the temple. Today, they would bury her father and huge crowds of people would stand on these very steps and pay their final respects to a king they'd loved so greatly. Of course, she would be there too but she also wanted to spend a few final moments with her father alone. She wanted to sit at his side and speak to him one more time without anyone else to hear what she had to say. As quietly as she possibly could, Brightness began to move towards the temple, her legs growing weary as she approached the top. When she finally did so, something brushed past her back and she gasped. Spinning her body around sharply, she saw a bat drifting away into the darkness. She breathed a sigh of relief. Resting for a moment, she looked down at the city below. It seemed so quiet but beyond the walls lay thousands of her uncle's warriors, ready to tear it down if he gave the word.

For a while, she sat there, looking up at the flickering stars. In her city, it was believed that once a great ruler had died, then they themselves would join the gods and watch over them. Brightness liked to think that was true. A warrior pure of heart, her father would serve the Lords of the skies well. She couldn't wait much longer. There would be no time. Creeping inside the walls of the temple, she felt a lump form in her throat. A lone flame partially lighting the room, she saw that her father's body had been laid flat on a stone table that stood in the centre of the room, a thin, red cotton cloth, covering the bottom half of his body. Her bare feet hardly making a sound, Brightness approached him, unable to resist brushing her hand softly against the cold skin of his forehead and resting it there on his temple. It was if he was asleep, she thought to herself, so peaceful lying there as if he were winding his way through a vivid dream.

"I love you father," she said, her eyes filling with hot tears. "Your spirit will shine amongst the stars."

Apart from a small scratch beneath his left eye, there were no visible marks upon his face or his upper torso. This left Brightness puzzled. She remembered clearly how he'd suddenly weakened during the battle with her uncle but she couldn't recall seeing an injury of any sort. Of course, from high above the city's walls, the two small figures below had often become a blur of swinging arms and whirling clubs. It had been difficult to see if any telling blow had been landed. Half-dreading what she would see, but allowing her curiosity to get the better of her, she began to move her hand down her father's neck and onto his chest, ready to slide the red cotton sheet away. Just before she did so, she heard footsteps. Someone was coming up the steps. Instinctively, she crept into the shadows, hiding behind the large pillar at the rear end of the room.

It wasn't long before a large figure stood at the entrance to the temple. Poking her head out as far as she dared, Brightness saw the High-Priest enter the room, so tall that the dark feathers of his headdress brushed against the ceiling. In the dim light, his eyes looked darker and more dangerous than ever. He towered there in the doorway for a while, not moving immediately, before eventually he moved towards her father's body. From somewhere within his robes, he took out a large knife, its sharp blade gleaming through the darkness. Brightness felt her heart beginning to thunder within her chest as he lay it down on the table so that it rested a short distance from her father's neck. What was the priest planning to do? She watched him place a huge hand on top of her father's ribs, stretching out his fingers and pressing them into his skin. Time and time again, he repeated this process, almost as if he was searching for the perfect spot. Brightness watched the priest's face as he stood at the stone table, his eyes cold and emotionless. Finally, he reached down and picked up the knife in his right hand, holding it directly above Blazing Sky's chest.

Brightness could wait no longer.

"Stop," she said firmly, stepping from the shadows. "Stop and explain yourself."

Startled, the High Priest stepped back, placing the knife back within his robes.

"My Princess," he said, forcing a smile so that the jade gems that lined his cracked teeth were visible, "You should not be here. This is not a place for young girls. It is here that I speak with the gods."

Summoning all of her courage, Brightness looked the priest right in the eye, trying not to let him see how afraid she was of him.

"He was my father and it is my right to be with him, either in life or in death," she said. "If that offends the gods then let them strike me from this Earth."

The High-Priest smiled again.

"As you wish my Princess but you have a long day ahead of you tomorrow," he said. "Your mother would not want you to spend the night out here."

"No, but she would not want me to leave him here alone so that you can do what you want with his body. I saw you about to cut him."

The High-Priest took a step forward towards Brightness and took out his knife once more.

"Do I frighten you Princess?" he asked.

She didn't answer at once, her eyes flicking between Blazing Sky's body and the knife.

"Yes," she said, "you do, but my father always told me that I should dismiss fear from my heart."

"Your father spoke many wise words," the High-Priest said, "and you have no reason to be frightened of me. With this knife, I seek to make the smallest of cuts. The royal blood that lies in his veins will please the gods when I offer it to them."

Brightness glared back at him, surprised at her own fierceness.

"His blood is not yours to give," she said, "and I order you to leave. I will stay with him until the first rays of light arrive."

They locked eyes for a time before finally the priest turned towards the exit. "As you wish Princess," he said coldly.

Chapter Ten

Don't Forget Me

Brightness stood with her mother at the foot of the tomb, a pyramid structure with nine stepped platforms, one for each layer of the underworld. Together, they watched her father's casket approaching, carried by Sunfire and five of the city's bravest warriors. Solemnly, they moved through the crowds of silent, sorrowful faces that lined the path they walked until finally they reached the stone walls. It was not since she had been a very young girl, that Brightness had been inside, when they'd buried her grandmother. Her grandfather's bones lay inside too, although he had passed away before she was born.

Inside the pyramid, it was pitch-black, only the flames of a flickering torch offering any respite from the darkness. They only needed to walk a short distance before arriving in what would be Blazing Sky's final resting place, a small room next to the tombs of his own parents. His body would now be close to them for eternity. Gently, they lowered his body into the stone sarcophagus. Throughout the night, carvers had worked, decorating it with images of their king and his ancestors being reborn as trees of the forest. Even at a time like this, Brightness couldn't help admiring the beauty of their work.

Under the watchful eye of the High-Priest, she watched her mother kiss her husband softly on the forehead before hanging an intricately designed necklace around his neck, while Sunfire lay his war club alongside him and rested his shield upon his midriff. Next, they spread a jaguar skin over the cotton cloth that wrapped around the body and placed maize within his mouth. He would need food for his journey to the afterlife.

Brightness looked down at her father. This would be the last time that she would see his face. Feeling an arm wrapping around her shoulder, she turned.

"His soul may be parted from his body," Sunfire whispered into her ear, "but from the other world he will be watching us. His spirit will live on and from the skies he will guide us."

Brightness nodded sadly. In her hands, she held a final gift to give to her father for his final journey. Skilfully fashioned from precious jade, she placed the mask over his face. Strangely beautiful in its own way, this item would grant a king a position amongst the gods. It was believed that those who wore it would be gifted a form of eternal life.

"Our great king is now ready to depart this world," the High-Priest said, the glowing flames of the candle lighting his face. "May his strength and wisdom continue to guide those who he leaves behind and let the Lords of the skies welcome him with open eyes."

He motioned to the warriors standing amongst the shadows at the back of the room. They stepped forward, carrying the huge rectangular slab of stone that would slide over the sarcophagus. It took twelve of them, muscles straining from their exertions, to lift it into place, sliding it over Blazing Sky's body and covering him for eternity. Brightness closed her eyes for a moment, trying to control her rapid breaths, only opening them when she felt Sunfire squeeze her hand.

Together, they looked down at the magnificent, artistic carvings on the lid. It showed her father at the centre of the universe, being reborn as a god, a cosmic tree leading him from the Earth to the skies. Blazing Sky had ordered work to begin on the design many years ago for it was not uncommon for a king to make the preparations for their own funeral. The time had come to leave, and with their hearts consumed with sorrow, they made their way outside. The walls to Blazing Sky's tomb would now be sealed forever.

There was little time for Brightness to mourn her father. On their return to their chambers, the High-Priest was waiting outside.

"Dark Eyes is ready to leave," he told the Queen. "He and his men have a long march ahead and they await your son outside the city's walls."

"Then Dark Eyes must wait longer," Brightness heard her mother reply. "My son has just buried his father. He will not leave until the sun next rises."

The High-Priest's cold eyes flickered ever so slightly.

"My Queen," he said, "Dark Eyes has spoken. If you refuse his request, then the peace that you have agreed may be broken."

The Queen remained unmoved, her face proud and strong.

"Tell Dark Eyes that I will be at the gates shortly," Sunfire said, looking at his mother before stepping forward. "Allow me a small amount of time with my mother and sister and then I will be at his side, ready to join him in Tikal."

The High-Priest waited for a moment, seeing that the Queen made no further protestations.

"I will tell Dark Eyes," he said.

Sunfire didn't have long, collecting only what was necessary for the journey ahead. As he did so Brightness waited at the entrance to his chambers.

"Sunfire," she said, her eyes consumed with anxiety, "I do not trust our uncle's word. How do we know he won't kill you the first chance he gets?"

"We don't – but for now we have no choice," he replied. "Dark Eyes is strong and now is not the time for our city to confront him. Our people will remember what he has done though. I will remember what he has done. I won't ever forget."

He stood beside her in the doorway now and they embraced.

"Sunfire," she asked him quietly. "Did you see our father suffer a wound when he fought?"

"I did not," he said, "nothing that was clear but Dark Eyes must have struck him. Everyone could see him weaken before our eyes. From so far away, it was difficult to see."

She held him tightly, not ever wanting to let go.

"I visited Father's body in the temple," she told him. "There wasn't more than a scratch on his body – not that I could see."

Sunfire looked down at his sister and smiled gently. "Brightness, our father died in battle, with honour. It doesn't matter if we didn't see the blow that killed him. His journey has taken him to the skies now and we cannot bring him back. Focus your thoughts on helping our mother rule this great city. She will need you by her side when I am gone."

He let her go and walked through the door, turning a final time.

"I will see you again Sister. Don't forget me."

Brightness and her mother followed Sunfire to the gates. On the Queen's signal, they opened and they saw her uncle waiting, standing in almost the exact spot he had slain Blazing Sky the previous day. Brightness felt her legs trembling as she remembered her father lying in the dust, his body motionless. The High-Priest stood at her uncle's side, watching closely as Sunfire embraced the Queen before walking away. Dark Eyes smiled as he approached, waiting in place as two of his warriors escorted the boy away from the city walls and beyond the first trees of the forest.

"Your son will serve Tikal well," he called out. "Your priest too.

Brightness stared at the High-Priest, the cogs in her head whirring away.

"The gods have spoken to me," the priest told the Queen. "I will serve them from the great city of Tikal now. A new path has been chosen for me. I will take care of your son and keep him safe."

Chapter Eleven

Injustice – I Can Feel It In My Heart

When darkness fell that night, Brightness found herself unable to sleep again. In the days that had passed, her world had broken apart, her mind overcome with a mixture of sorrow and fury. She vowed that her uncle would pay for what he had done. Maybe not today or tomorrow, maybe not until a great deal of time had passed, but he would suffer one day. She wanted him to feel the pain that she had done. Only then could she rest. She thought about the High-Priest too. She was glad that he was gone but there were answers that she wanted from him too. She was sure that he knew more about her father's death than he was letting on. Racking her brains, she tried to play through the sequence of events in her mind. She remembered the speed of her father's footwork as he'd ducked and swayed away from her uncle's murderous swings and how her heart had fluttered each time the club had thumped into his shield. She recalled the deafening cracking sound that had erupted when Dark Eyes weapon had splintered in his hands and how his eyes had betrayed the fear he had felt. He had known that he was staring death in the face. But then something had changed. Her father, once so agile, had become heavy-footed, each movement forced and painful to watch. Had he been wounded? The more she thought about it, the less she believed it to be true. She had not seen Dark Eyes land a single blow upon her father's flesh and seeing his body, lying unmarked within the temple, only reinforced this point of view. Whatever had happened, the High-Priest had something to do with it. She pictured him towering over her father's body, eyes cold and lifeless, knife in hand. What had he been planning before she'd surprised him? He'd certainly been quick enough to follow her uncle back to Tikal. Brightness didn't trust either of them and doubted their promise of peace would be upheld. Something told her that Sunfire would not be allowed to live out his days in Tikal and that Dark Eyes and the High-Priest had another fate in mind for him. She waited there until the morning thinking about nothing else.

The following day, as the first rays of light streaked through the forest, Brightness made her way out of their chambers, telling her mother that she was going hunting. She had no such intention, travelling instead to the Eastern walls of the city where a small farmhouse stood. Outside, a woman sat beside a fire, the smoke drifting up into the clear blue skies of the morning.

"Princess," she said. "Would you like some food?"

Brightness shook her head. Though the smell wafting up from the pot was intoxicating, at this time she had no interest in eating.

"Princess, I am sorry that your father has left this Earth," the woman continued. "I pray that he will guide our city from the heavens as wisely as he did while he lived."

Brightness smiled at her sadly, her lips trembling slightly and unable to reply.

"My son lies inside," the woman said. "It will please him to see you."

Nodding a response, Brightness entered the farmhouse. Inside it was quite spacious, large enough to fit six hammocks that hung across its mid-section and still leave room for a variety of ceramic pots that were used for cooking, storing grain and carrying water. The walls themselves were constructed from wooden strips that had been woven together and fixed in place using mud and clay while in the very centre of the home was a fireplace marked by three large hearthstones. In the very last hammock, a figure lay, turning as Brightness made her way towards him.

"Princess," Flint-Knife said, wincing as he began to sit upright. "You should be with your family. They will need you at your home."

Brightness looked down at the injured boy, seeing that although the graze on his cheek had begun to heal, his rib cage was an angry purple. He saw her staring and forced a smile.

"You may have to find a new partner for the next ball game," he said. "I fear my bones are too old for such activities."

Brightness managed a small smile herself.

"My friend, I have buried my father and my mother is the only family I have left at my home," she told him, "I will return to her shortly, but my brother needs me more than ever. I fear his life is in great danger and I am sure my uncle will soon kill him. He cares little about his words of peace."

Flint-Knife looked up, seeing the urgency in her eyes. It worried him.

"How can you be certain of his intentions Princess? Our city has little choice but to take the word of Dark Eyes."

"I can not prove anything," she said, "but I can feel it in my heart that my father suffered a great injustice."

"What do you mean Princess?" Flint-Knife asked. "A battle was fought and your uncle was the victor. This cannot be changed."

She told him everything – how her father had suddenly weakened with no obvious wound, how she'd seen the High-Priest in the temple, ready to cut into her father's flesh, how he now served her uncle. When she had finished, she found her hands shaking. Flint-Knife took them gently in his own.

"We must tell the Queen of what you suspect," he said softly. "She will send an army of warriors to return your brother to us. We will free him or die trying."

Brightness shook her head. "I will not make my mother send men to their deaths while I have no proof of my uncle's deception," she said. "My father gave his life so that our people would be free from the threat of war. I won't dishonour him by starting one."

"Then what will you do?"

"When I leave here," she said, "I will enter the forests and follow my uncle's men. If I move quickly then I will catch them before the sun falls. I will see with my own eyes what the priest plans for my brother."

She paused for a moment before continuing.

"Will you help me my friend?" she asked, squeezing his fingers gently.

He nodded his agreement.

"I want you to go to my mother and tell her that I plan to follow my brother to Tikal. By then I will be long gone. Tell her that I only plan to see that he has arrived safely and then I will return. You will offer your services to her. She knows that you are not only a skilled tracker but loyal and trustworthy too."

"So loyal that I should tell a story to my Queen. Men have been put to death for less," Flint-Knife interrupted, stopping Brightness in her tracks. He'd caught her a little off-guard.

"To tell a small lie for your Princess does not blacken your heart my friend," she said, "and what you tell my mother will be true."

"I will not be giving her the whole story," he said, stone-faced.

Brightness felt a small prickle of guilt but dismissed it as quickly as it entered her head.

"But that is different from lying," she said, a little anger rising in her chest, "and the gods should only frown upon a lie if the person's intentions are not pure."

Flint-Knife smiled at last. "Princess," he said playfully. "It will be a great honour to tell a small lie for you."

Brightness couldn't suppress a slight giggle.

"You must convince my mother that you can reach me quickly and return me to the city."

"Princess," I can't convince my own body that I can move quickly," he said looking down at his swollen ribs.

"Then you will tell the Queen two small lies," Brightness smiled, "and show that you are strong enough to call yourself a warrior of this city."

She continued. "After you have done so, you will tell her that you will return me safely to Dos Pilas. She will want to send more men but you will make her see that more men increases the chance of being seen. If Dark Eyes catches even a glimpse of our warriors then our peace will already be broken. My mother will know this. Promise her that you will return with me by your side and then follow me into the forests. I will wait for you by the river."

"It sounds as if you have given this much thought Princess," Flint-Knife said. "I will do all that you ask of me but tell me, what will you do once we have reached your brother?"

Brightness stared back at him, not sure of the answer to this question herself.

"When I lie beneath the stars tonight, I will look up to the skies and pray," she said. "If my father truly belongs to the gods, he will guide me."

Chapter Twelve

A Cry From The Blackness

Brightness made her way through the thick walls of the forest until she found herself at the river's edge, moving out from the shade of the trees and into the early evening sunlight. Here, she waited for Flint-Knife's arrival, watching the turtles sunning themselves on the rocks. Her head, clouded so heavily by all she had endured, began to clear as she looked up at the birds in the trees. There were colourful macaws, sporting bright red feathers and wings tipped with blue, as well as a row of three yellow-bellied flycatchers singing away noisily at each other. How bright and cheerful they seemed, without a care in the world. How she wished that she could enjoy life as much as they seemed to. Her eyes followed the path of the river, as it twisted away North, swallowed up by a dense jungle so lush and unspoiled. Somewhere up ahead, her uncle's men made their way back to Tikal, taking Sunfire with them. Her body overcome with exhaustion, having hardly slept during the days that had passed, she lay back against the rocks and closed her eyes, not even disturbed by the shrills howls of the monkeys that rose above the gentle hum of the insects.

As Brightness dreamt, she pictured her father's face, proud and strong as he stood outside the walls of his city. She found herself walking towards him but as she reached out a hand to him, his body changed form and became that of an eagle, soaring up into the skies until it became no more than a small dot amongst

the clouds. She kept her eyes firmly fixed upon the
bird, only turning when it had completely disappeared
from view. As she did so, she looked up at the temple
that towered above the city walls. Straining her eyes,
she tried to make out the two figures that stood at the
top of its steps. Finally, their faces became clear. The
closer of the two was her brother, Sunfire, while behind
him stood the tall figure of the High-Priest holding a
gleaming blade.

"Princess," she heard a distant voice calling.
"Princess, wake up."

Stirred from her slumbers, she awoke to see Flint-
Knife smiling down at her.

"So," he said, "those with royal blood do snore
too. How do you propose that we creep amongst your
uncle's men while you make such a noise?"

She rubbed away the sleep from her eyes.

"I'd never have thought that a princess would make
such a dreadful sound," he continued to tease.

"There are many things about me that you wouldn't
think I'd do," Brightness replied, "like cut a boy's
throat when he insults me."

She smiled, enjoying her own response. "What has
taken you long? I hope you are not going to blame sore
ribs for your lack of haste."

"Your eyes may be drowsy but your tongue is still
sharp," he said. "And the pain within my ribs is easing.
Thank you for your concern."

Flint-Knife had brought some food with him and
they ate while they walked. They would still be some
way behind her uncle but if they moved quickly they
might catch up with them by nightfall. Having not had
a meal for some time, Brightness ate hungrily, chewing

away at the meat from a quail and nibbling at fresh corn
as they walked along the bank of the river. Suddenly,
she stopped dead in her tracks, gripping Flint-Knife's
hand and pressing a finger to her lips. High up in the
trees that hung over the water, she pointed to a jaguar
inching its way across the branches, the spotted patterns
of its beautiful fur only just visible against the bark,
eyes firmly fixed upon a spider monkey that sat picking
a handful of berries and stuffing them into its mouth.
Closer and closer, it moved. It occurred to Brightness
that she and Flint-Knife could take a lesson from this
creature. They too would need to move with cunning,
remaining out of sight until the right moment presented
itself. Then, when the time was right, they'd make their
move. Sadly, unlike the jaguar, she wasn't certain of
what that move would be. Taking a small pebble from
the river bank, she aimed it in the spider monkey's
direction. Striking the branch with a sharp crack, it was
enough to send the monkey scurrying away and out
of reach of the large cat. Brightness and Flint-Knife
watched from a safe distance as it slunk its way back to
the forest floor, springing away into the trees.

Although they moved as quickly as they could, by
nightfall, they still hadn't caught up with Dark Eyes
and his men. Brightness could see that Flint-Knife's
movement was still impaired by his injury and felt a
tinge of regret that she had teased him about it earlier.
With every step that he took, she saw him wince with
pain and it was clear that he would not be able to walk
for much longer.

"We should stop and rest for the night," she said.
"My feet are sore and my legs ache. At first light, we
can begin moving again."

Flint-Knife nodded his approval, too exhausted to answer.

"We will take turns to sleep," she continued, remembering the jaguar creeping its way towards the spider monkey. "Give me your bow and I will watch first."

He was too tired to argue, sitting down with his back resting against a large tree and falling asleep almost immediately after he had closed his eyes.

Brightness sat opposite him, bow in hand, her long hunting knife tucked within her belt, ready to draw it if needed. There were many predators within the forest, not just jaguars but a great variety of snakes and ocelots too. Under the light of a small flame, she kept a sharp eye out for any slight movement amongst the trees. At one point, she thought she heard something rustling against the leaves and leapt to her feet with bow drawn back and ready to release an arrow, a wave of relief washing over her body when nothing more than an inquisitive porcupine emerged. Although she hated to admit it, being in the darkness had always made her feel uncomfortable. She didn't enjoy sitting there, surrounded by dense forest, not knowing what eyes were watching her. Even when the time came for her to switch roles with Flint-Knife and take her turn to rest, she was reluctant to do so, not sure she if she could sleep anyway. In her mind, she tried to play through what she would do when they eventually caught up with Dark Eyes and his men. It was not as if she and Flint-Knife could simply leap from the cover of the trees and confront an entire army of warriors. Could they find a way of freeing Sunfire? Maybe. If they could somehow stay hidden, an opportunity may present itself once darkness had fallen. She found herself dismissing this thought too. Sunfire wasn't really a prisoner. He had left Dos Pilas, perhaps not of his own free will, but as part of the peace agreement. If he just suddenly disappeared then Dark Eyes would have the perfect excuse to turn his army around and burn Dos Pilas to the ground. She grew restless as she realised that there was no perfect plan and she didn't know what she would do, becoming overwhelmed at the thought of her brother coming to any harm. How lonely he must feel, torn away from his family and forced to live in a city of strangers. If they decided to let him live at all.

Brightness slumped back against a tree, growing tired now and looking over at Flint-Knife sleeping peacefully. For a moment, she considered waking him, but remembering how pained and exhausted his movements had been as he'd struggled through the forest, she decided against it. Ill at ease and agitated, she picked at her fingers, scratching away the grime that had collected beneath her fingernails, disturbed occasionally by the odd hoot or howl. Eventually, allowing her muscles to relax, she managed to calm herself down. She couldn't let her emotions cloud her head for she would need a clear mind to help her brother. Without realising how tired she'd become, her eyelids began to grow heavy and close.

Crack! The angry sound of a branch snapping awoke her followed by a muffled cry. Springing quickly to her feet, she held the candle before her face. While she'd slept, the flame had almost died out and it was difficult to see in the gloom. Through the darkness, she crept forward, light in one hand, dagger in the other.

"Flint-Knife," she half whispered. "Where are you?"

He didn't respond but she thought that she heard a movement from the trees in front of her. Taking a further step forward, she felt her foot catch on something and she stumbled onto one knee, just about holding on the candle but releasing her grip on the dagger. She heard it thump into the ground, some distance away and out of sight. Another muffled cry came from somewhere in the blackness, much closer now. Brightness rose to her feet. She could hear the sound of her own breath now, strained and anxious. She lifted the candle up before her eyes so that she could see more clearly, unsure whether she should search for her knife or continue onwards unarmed.

"Flint-Knife," she called once more, forcing her unwilling legs to move. Then, recoiling in horror, she saw him, slumped back against the tree she'd left him sleeping against, the elongated form of a large snake, wrapped around his neck. Instinctively she thrust her body into action, lunging forward and grabbing frantically at its muscular body in an effort to free Flint-Knife from its vice-like hold. Coiled around the boy, it had completely enveloped his chest and neck, attempting to close off his windpipe and squeeze the air from his lungs. In desperation, she beat her fists against its neck, aware of Flint-Knife's desperate breaths as his own arms flailed away beside her. A raw panic threatened to overwhelm her, rising up through her chest as she locked eyes with him. She knew, without any shadow of a doubt, that this huge snake would relentlessly increase the pressure it put on him unless she could do something to stop it but as hard as she pounded at its skin, it wouldn't loosen its grip. If it continued for much longer then Flint-Knife would die of suffocation.

Abandoning her assault for a moment, Brightness swung away to her left so that she came face to face with the snake, seeing its cold, merciless eyes for the first time. Reaching for a piece of loose branch that lay on the ground, as quick as a flash, she brought it down upon the creature's nostrils with as much force as she could summon. This time the snake did react, suddenly jerking forward violently, jaws wide and fangs gleaming. Too quick for Brightness to avoid, its fearsome teeth approached her unguarded face until she felt them sear into her cheek. The pain was excruciating, far worse than she remembered when she'd been bitten as a little girl. It was as if a collection of small, sharp knives had pierced her flesh. Thrashing out wildly with her stick, she succeeded in alarming the snake enough that it retracted its head as quickly as it had attacked, disentangling itself from both Flint-Knife and the tree. Briefly it retreated, uncoiling itself so that it was possible to see just how long its body was, stretching out upon the forest floor, easily the length of three grown men. The side of her face throbbing, Brightness watched it cautiously, feeling a steady flow of warm, sticky blood ooze from her cheek. There was no time to feel sorry for herself as she saw the snake turn its body and face her once more, rearing its head angrily as if ready to strike. She in turn lifted her stick although it now seemed pitifully small. For a while they eyed each other, neither prepared to move first. Brightness was aware of Flint-Knife lying behind her but as much as she wanted to, she daren't risk a glance to check on his condition. Finally, the snake lunged towards her but this time she was ready for it, swaying out of range of its teeth and jabbing out her stick into the side of the creature's neck. To her surprise, this seemed to deter it, for it quickly slunk away into the foliage, unwilling to risk another attack.

Breathing heavily, she watched the last of its body disappear from view, sinking to her knees in relief for a moment before turning and running to Flint-Knife's side. When she saw him rising gingerly to his feet, her heart leapt and without thinking she wrapped her arms around him.

"I'm sorry," she said, "I fell asleep. I'm sorry."

He flinched sharply, and remembering his blackened ribs, she released her grip immediately. She felt her cheeks burning, embarrassed that she'd caused him further pain and that she'd embraced him with such affection.

"Princess," he scolded lightly, his voice shaky and struggling to breathe, "first the snake and now you. My ribs have never endured such suffering." He tried smiling but it ended up turning into more of a grimace and before Brightness could catch hold of him, he fell to one knee.

She took his hand and helped him rest back against the tree once more, easing her bottle of water to his lips.

"Should you check that there's nothing in the branches this time?" he asked. She couldn't help her lips spreading into a small smile, glancing up into the tree and covering her mouth in mock horror.

"I am sorry Flint-Knife," she repeated. The boy, normally so strong and athletic, seemed to have visibly weakened before her eyes. "Can you forgive me?"

He squeezed her hand and nodded. "Are you hurt Princess?" he asked.

Her face. In her joy at finding Flint-Knife alive, she'd ignored the pain coming from her cheek. Gingerly, she lifted her fingers to the wound, feeling the blood still trickling down her face."

"My face will be marked?" she asked him sadly. "It will remind me of my stupidity."

Flint-Knife studied her face, seeing how the snake had sunk its teeth into her flesh.

"No Princess," he said. "It will remind me of your courage."

Chapter Thirteen

Trust Me

Neither Brightness or Flint-Knife dared close their eyes for the rest of the night and at as the first rays of light streamed through the trees, he stumbled to his feet.

"We should walk," he said. "Your uncle will soon be marching."

She looked up at him, seeing the exhaustion in his eyes. Rising to her feet, she took him by the arm, guiding his unsteady legs back to the tree he'd rested upon.

"You are too weak to move," she told him firmly, "and you must rest. "I will go on alone from here."

She paused waiting for a response, knowing that he would argue with her. His face, usually so full of warmth, betrayed the slightest hint of anger. She had wounded his pride.

"My place is by your side Princess," he said, "I will cover myself in shame if I leave you."

"My friend, you would not be leaving me – I would be leaving you. There would be no shame in that."

He wouldn't take no for an answer. "I will not slow you down Princess," he promised her, "and I will not return to our city without you. I will die before that happens."

She hesitated for a moment and sighed. She knew how stubborn Flint-Knife could be.

"Princess," he told her, "If a large snake could not crush me, then a walk through the forest will be easy. You'll see. I will move with the speed and grace of a jaguar. You will beg me to slow down."

She laughed and relented. "You weren't quicker than me before you hurt your ribs and you will not be when they are healed but yes, we will travel on together if you give me your word."

"My word?" he asked.

"You will give me your word that first you will rest while I look for some food. We will need more than rice and beans to give us strength."

It didn't take Brightness long before she'd reached the river. The sun was beginning to rise and spread its warmth. Keeping a watchful eye on a crocodile that lay, almost fully submerged, within the water on the opposite side of the river, she washed her face, wincing as she washed the dried blood from the bite on her cheek. Studying her reflection while she knelt on the bank, she saw the swollen red welts where the snake's teeth had pierced her skin and grimaced, tracing a finger over them tenderly. In time, they'd heal but there would always be a scar to remind her of the unwanted encounter. Turning away, she moved back into the cover of the trees. This was no time to feel sorry for herself. There were far greater things to worry about than her face.

Returning to the edge of the forest, she climbed up into the branches of the trees, Flint-Knife's bow hanging at her waist. With morning breaking, it wouldn't be long before animals came to quench their thirst. Her eyes fixed on the river bank, she lifted an arrow into place, ready to send it whistling through the air. The bow itself, was beautiful in its own way and Brightness knew how proud Flint-Knife was of it. A gift from his father, it had been fashioned from the finest wood, with incredibly detailed patterns carved into its side. It seemed strange that something that had been forged with such love and care could be used to bring death but once the volcanic glass tip, dipped in secreted frog poison, had pierced the flesh of a victim, the life would begin to drain from their body. As she sat there, the bow pointed at the riverside, she thought of sending such an arrow into her uncle's neck.

It wasn't long before she was back at Flint-Knife's side, fashioning a meal from the meat of a tapir that she'd killed, cutting away strips of flesh and adding them to the rice and beans that he'd brought with him for the journey. They both ate hungrily and for a while Brightness, comforted by a full stomach, managed to forget the awfulness of the past few days or at least push it to the back of her mind. She shared some berries that she'd collected and enjoyed their sweet taste as she popped them in her mouth. If it were not for the ordeals that they'd suffered through and the troubles that would soon face them, then it could have been a perfect day, with the thin beams of sunlight amongst the shadows making the forest even more beautiful.

As much as Brightness had enjoyed sitting and eating, she knew that they could rest no longer. Her uncle's men would soon be on the move and they'd have to move quickly if they were to catch them by nightfall. At least the meal seemed to have done Flint-Knife good and if anything, he seemed to be moving better than yesterday. For the rest of the morning, they alternated between jogging and walking and not once did he complain about the pain his ribs must have been causing him. Stopping only to take on water, they moved at a good pace only slowing when the trees became so tightly packed together that it was difficult to squeeze between them. As they moved, Flint-Knife grew more excitable, identifying the route that Dark Eyes and his men must have trodden, seeing the markings their boots had made and the places in which their blades had cut back the thicker parts of the jungle. It was almost as if the thrill of the chase had rejuvenated him.

Twilight was just beginning to close in when they heard the first voices. Flint-Knife stopped dead in his tracks. They both knew that they mustn't get too close just yet and any quick movement could alert Dark Eyes' men. Every step they now made would need to be taken with care. From a safe distance, they followed, occasionally catching sight of the warriors that brought up the rear of the march. At one point, Brightness trod clumsily upon a broken branch, snapping it in two. Frozen to the spot, she held her breath but although they stopped momentarily, not one of her uncle's warriors turned to investigate the noise she had made. Fortunately, the trees in this part of the forest had grown thicker once more, helping conceal them from view. Brightness felt a wave of relief wash over her as she watched the men move on unaware, possibly dismissing the cracked branch as animals moving amongst the undergrowth. She tried not to steal a glance at Flint-Knife, knowing that he was silently admonishing her. Her cheeks crimson, they continued their pursuit.

Their feet sore and muscles aching, Brightness and Flint-Knife followed Dark Eyes' army through the forest until darkness finally began to swallow up the trees. They still hadn't caught a glimpse of Sunfire but he'd be out there somewhere, hidden amongst the

swarm of men. Eventually, the procession of warriors
came to a sharp halt, setting up camp for the night
in a bit of a clearing where the trees had thinned out
a little. Brightness watched through the gloom as a
good number of them scuffled about collecting loose
branches and twigs to make a series of small fires. It
wasn't long before the flames began to illuminate the
blackness, allowing her to see the faces of the men
who sat in the warmth, enjoying a mouthful of food
after a long day of walking. Turning to Flint-Knife, she
pointed upwards into the trees and pressed a finger to
her lips. He nodded and together they climbed high up
into the trees that surrounded the clearing, hidden by
the branches.

Picking their spot carefully, they settled in against
the trunk, well concealed but able to peer down upon
the army of men that rested below them. As night drew
in, the air had cooled considerably and Brightness
was grateful for the heat that drifted up from the fires.
She reached for the water that she'd carried with her,
offering some to Flint-Knife before gulping down a
few mouthfuls herself. Looking down at the sea of
fierce faces, each one hardened from many battles,
she felt the blood surging through her veins. Neither
she nor Flint-Knife could make a sound or they'd give
themselves away and then what would happen? Would
a series of arrows soar up in their direction and dig into
their flesh? Would men climb up towards them, axes
at the ready? She remembered how clumsy she'd been
when treading on the broken branch and forced herself
to concentrate. One stupid move could get them both
killed. Silently she racked her brains. What should she
do? It was not as if she could simply climb down and
demand to see her brother. Such foolishness would

embarrass her. Helpless as she now felt, she began to question the wisdom of what she had done. She'd set off after her uncle clouded by emotion, her heart ruling her head, not really having any real plan of what she would do and dragging poor Flint-Knife and his damaged ribs along too. Her mother would be furious with her when she found out. Feeling sorry for herself, she ran the palms of her hands down her forehead and covered her eyes, flinching as her fingers brushed against the wound on her cheek.

"Princess," she heard Flint-Knife whisper, breaking her out from her thoughts, his voice barely audible.

She turned towards him and saw him pointing to her left, his eyes fixed upon the far side of the clearing. Straining her eyes through the smoke that drifted up from the fires, she saw Sunfire, his jaguar headdress instantly recognisable, even from some distance away. Sitting beside the High-Priest, he didn't appear to have been mistreated in any way, tucking in hungrily to the bowls of food that were being passed around. He didn't look like anyone's prisoner. Perhaps her uncle was going to be true to his word after all and treat Sunfire honourably. To her surprise, she found herself feeling a little deflated at this. Of course, she didn't want to see her brother come to any harm but it also left her feeling a little humiliated having rushed off with the intention of rescuing her brother from some sort of terrible fate, only to see that he was in no danger whatsoever. She felt a prod in her ribs and saw that Flint-Knife was gesturing at her to follow him. Obediently, she did so, manoeuvring her way from tree to tree, taking great care with each soundless step until eventually, without too much difficulty they had positioned themselves so they were directly above Sunfire, too high up to be visible but close enough to be within earshot. Breathlessly, they listened to him talking with the High-Priest.

"Your uncle will treat you as if you are a Prince of Tikal," the High-Priest told Sunfire. "You will have everything that you desire. The best food, the most comfortable sleeping quarters, there is nothing that you cannot have."

"Except my family," Sunfire replied, not looking up from his bowl.

The High-Priest stopped talking for a while, taking a mouthful of food himself.

"It is true that you have suffered," he said, "but in time your mother and sister may be allowed to visit you in Tikal. Until then, you should live your life in the best way you can. They would not want you to be unhappy."

Sunfire shook his head, a slight trace of anger on his face.

"There is no amount of wealth that can bring back my father," he said. "No matter how rich the food that I eat tastes or how fine the clothes that I'll wear are, I won't forget that my uncle murdered him."

"Your uncle and your father chose to settle their differences on the battlefield," replied the High-Priest. "You would be wise to remember that rather than talk with a loose tongue."

Brightness watched Sunfire glare back at the High-Priest, defiant in the face of this rebuke.

"I didn't trust you when you served my father," he said quietly. "I didn't like you then and I don't like you now. You don't serve the gods – you serve yourself."

With that, Sunfire rose to his feet.

"I am tired and need to rest," he said. "Tell me where I should lie."

Glancing behind him at a warrior, who stood watching Sunfire's every move, the High-Priest nodded.

"This man will watch you as you sleep," he said pausing a while. "To make sure nothing happens to you," he added icily.

Brightness watched her brother disappear from view. She was tired now herself and hungry too, Neither she nor Flint-Knife had eaten since the morning but the rice and beans that he'd carried had long since been finished off along with the strips of tapir meat. She had to be content with the last few berries that she'd collected, sharing the meagre amount with Flint-Knife and worrying that her growling stomach might alert her uncle's men to their position. She took a moment to consider her options. She'd seen her brother, and although she couldn't say he was unhappy, he hadn't been mistreated either. She and Flint-Knife could follow him all the way to Tikal but what use would that do? Perhaps it was time to return home before her mother lost patience and sent the warriors of Dos Pilas after her. She couldn't risk reigniting the war so quickly. As she contemplated this, she heard further movement below them, seeing a tall figure approaching the High-Priest. It was the unmistakable form of her uncle, his fierce face glowing in the firelight. She felt her heart quicken.

"My nephew looked angry," he said.

"He doesn't trust me. He probably doesn't trust you either," the High-Priest replied.

"Then the boy is no fool. I took his father's life. I've taken him from his family. Why should he trust me?"

The High-Priest nodded.

"When will he know of our plans for him my King?"

"We will tell him nothing for some time. It would not

be wise to provoke Dos Pilas so quickly. They would be ready and prepared for an attack. Why should I lose good men in battle when we can take their city when their guard is down? No, we will wait. Let the boy live amongst our people for a while at least."

The High-Priest smiled.

"The gods have granted you great wisdom my King," he said.

"In time," Dark-Eyes continued, "my nephew's blood will be spilt upon the ball court and glory will be showered upon Tikal. His defeat and sacrifice will bring strength to our people."

"Dos Pilas will not rest until his death has been avenged my King. The Queen would fight you until her dying breath."

Dark Eyes smiled cruelly before answering.

"As my nephew's blood flows down the steps of the city temple," he said, "my warriors will be at the gates of Dos Pilas. By the time the Queen learns of his death, her city will be ablaze."

Listening with horror, Brightness felt her fingers trembling so much that she worried that she would lose her grip on the branches and fall right out of the tree. She felt Flint-Knife place his hand on hers and turned to face him. He looked awful, his eyes wide and fearful. They were planning to kill Sunfire. Not right away but soon enough, and then once his blood had been offered to the gods, Dos Pilas would be reduced to ashes. Her worst fears had proven to be true. She knew she had to think clearly but what should she do? Every part of her wanted to run as fast as she could back to her mother and tell her what Dark Eyes planned to do with Sunfire. She would have their warriors march on Tikal immediately. This seemed like the right thing to do but something bothered her about this cause of action. Brave and skilled fighters though they were, the army of Dos Pilas would clearly be no match for the might of her uncle's kingdom, especially without her father to lead them. They would fight with courage, but greatly outnumbered, they would almost certainly be defeated. Sunfire would be killed anyway and Dos Pilas would be left unguarded. There had to be another way. For now though, she could do nothing as her uncle's men had surrounded the perimeter of the clearing, making any attempts to retreat back into the forest impossible. She and Flint-Knife would have to spend the night in the trees. Finding the thickest parts of the trunk that they could, they used their woven belts to strap themselves in place, for it would be easy to toss and turn within their sleep and plummet to the ground.

"This time you can sleep first," Flint-Knife whispered and she knew that it would be foolish to argue. Surprisingly, she found herself drifting towards sleep in next to no time, her tired limbs ignoring the discomfort of their sleeping arrangements.

When Flint-Knife eventually awoke her so that he could rest his own eyes, Brightness's head felt as clear as it had done for days. Even the short amount of rest had revived her weakening body. Sipping from the water bottle, she peered down at the fierce men that slept below, their shadowy shapes vague in the darkness that surrounded them. Her brother lay somewhere amongst them and she shuddered as she thought of her uncle's plans for him. After lying against the tree trunk, her back was a little sore so she turned and sat upright upon the branch keeping a careful eye on Flint-Knife as he slept and taking the occasional nervous glance at the branches above his head. As she did so, an idea struck her and the skin on her arms began to tingle. It would be terribly dangerous and she would be putting her own life at risk but it was the only way she could think of that would keep Sunfire alive and prevent her city from being burnt to the ground. No matter how much water she drank, her throat seemed to grow ever drier but however much it frightened her, she knew what she needed to do. "Do not let yourself become strangled with fear," she whispered softly to herself. "Show no cowardice. What use is your life if you have no family to share it with?"

She sat there alone until the sun began to rise, listening to the birds squawk out a morning greeting. She could see her uncle's men beginning to stir below her, a few beginning to light fires and prepare something to eat, some gathering up their weapons and various other belongings. Feeling frustrated, Brightness watched them bustle about, knowing that all she could do for now was sit and wait.

Eventually, Dark Eyes led his army from the clearing and ahead into the forest. It wouldn't take them too much longer to reach Tikal now, perhaps half a day of walking before they reached the outskirts of the great city. Brightness and Flint-Knife watched the last of them slip away from view, waiting impatiently in their tree top hiding place until they could be absolutely certain they were alone. Finally, they climbed down from their perch, glad to be on firm ground even if there was no time to rest their aching limbs.

"We should return to Dos Pilas before it is too late Princess," Flint-Knife urged, his face shrouded with concern. "The Queen must know what your uncle plans. Our warriors will soon be at the gates of Tikal."

He took a number of paces towards the edge of the

clearing, urgency in each of his steps.

"Wait," Brightness called after him and he stopped sharply, spinning to face her. She saw the confusion on his face.

"We can bring every warrior we have to Tikal and it will not save my brother's life. It will only bring forward his death."

He stared back at her, trying to make sense of what she was trying to tell him.

"Returning to Dos Pilas is not the way," she said assertively. "Can I ask you to trust me my friend?"

Chapter Fourteen

I Would Die For My Brother

Brightness had never felt so alone as she emerged from the jungle and stood before the great city of Tikal. It had taken her a while to convince Flint-Knife that her plan was the best of the limited options that were available but reluctantly he'd agreed. As strong as the anger she felt towards her uncle was, she couldn't help admire the majesty of the city he'd helped create. It had been many years since she'd set foot within its walls but seeing it through older eyes did not diminish the sense of wonder she felt as she stared up the magnificent temple of the two-headed serpent that towered up into the skies. Constructed with the intention of bringing those who climbed its steps closer to the gods, elaborate stone carvings of gods and mystical creatures covered the walls while endless steps led up towards its shrine. Surrounding this spectacular building were a number of smaller pyramids, although all of these were at least as tall of the grand temple of Dos Pilas, each one their own special testament to the gods, many of them holding the remains of kings and queens who had long since passed from this Earth. A far greater fate, Brightness thought morbidly to herself, than that which awaited her brother if she didn't act. The sacrifice of an enemy prince would be the most prized of offerings to the gods, particularly when performed as part of a ballgame ritual. A re-enactment of the beheading of the hero twins by the Lords of the underworld was one such monstrous story she'd heard took place under her uncle's rule of Tikal and knowing his cruelty, she was sure that it was true.

Steeling herself, Brightness approached the gates. From a high vantage point within the trees, she and Flint-Knife had watched the crowds gathering in the great plaza that stood beneath the temple of the serpents. When she'd been a small child, staying in Tikal with her father, she remembered how her uncle had paraded an enemy king he'd captured in battle, his 'prize' on display for the people of his city. It was a display of strength for a leader to do such a thing and Brightness had known there was a good chance that Sunfire would be brought to the plaza before the day had passed, not to be humiliated or threatened, but more as a way of showing the power that Dark Eyes held over all that opposed him. Sure enough, as the daylight began to fade, she and Flint-Knife had seen and heard the city's inhabitants bustling towards the plaza. A show was being prepared for them.

Her blood thundering through her veins, Brightness made her way towards the city, her body freezing when she heard the order to stop. Above her, she heard a bow being drawn back and she held her breath, knowing an arrow could pierce her heart at any moment. From within the huge wooden gates, two fearsome looking warriors stepped forward, each brandishing a macuahuitl, ready to swing it into her if given the slightest provocation. The taller of the two, his violent eyes studying the slight figure that dared to stand before him, reached out a muscular arm and grabbed Brightness around the collar. So strong was the grip he held her with, that she found herself balancing on one foot, the left side of her body being lifted off the floor. His face was pressed so close to hers that she could smell the foul stench of his breath and see the ugly scar that snaked its way down his right cheek.

"It's a little girl," he sneered contemptuously. "What business do you have in Tikal girl?"

Brightness tried to answer him but her words stuck in her mouth, unable to escape. Instead, an indecipherable mumble emerged from her lips.

"Well?" said the guard. "Tell me why I should not cut your throat and leave the birds to pick at your bones."

Now struggling to keep even one foot on the ground, Brightness tried to compose herself. Sunfire would need her to show that she was strong.

"I am the Princess of Dos Pilas," she said firmly. "And I am here to give a message to my uncle."

The man holding her was so surprised at this answer, especially at the authority within her voice, that he loosened his grip and allowed Brightness to stand with her two feet planted on the ground once more.

"You speak with a false tongue girl. I should cut it from your mouth," he told her, but Brightness could detect a level of uncertainty.

"It is true that a powerful warrior like you could remove my tongue if you wished," she said boldly, "but then my uncle would not receive the message I have for him. I know him well enough to say that he would show you little or no mercy if he found out that you had kept him from hearing what I have to say."

The warrior released his hold on Brightness altogether, although he glared at her angrily.

"How do I know that you are who you say and how

would the King find out that you had carried a message for him?" he said. "I could kill you and leave your body rotting in the forests without him ever knowing."

Dismissing thoughts of animals nibbling at her dead body, Brightness answered him without hesitation.

"My mother, Queen of Dos Pilas, has entrusted me to deliver my uncle's message. It must come from my lips and my lips alone. If I do not return safely within seven days then she will know that I have come to harm and inform my uncle that I have been killed unjustly."

"And the Queen would send her only daughter alone to Tikal?" he questioned.

"A number of her finest warriors travelled with me," she said. "They wait in the forests as my mother demanded that no form of aggression be displayed but they know that I have reached Tikal safely. If I disappear, my death will be traced back to those who guard the city gates."

She paused, watching the guard's face closely.

"Your head would look good on a spike," she said and though his face glowered with rage, she could sense his nervousness.

"We will take you to the King," he said. "Let us see what this message you have for him is. Follow me," he said. "Princess – and if you have been lying we will see whose head is on a spike."

It didn't take long until they reached the great plaza, pushing past the crowds that had packed themselves in below the temple's steps and settling into a position not far from the stone platform which had been raised up so that it overlooked the main square. Her heart sank a little as she saw the tall figure of Dark Eyes, with Sunfire stood awkwardly at his side. Addressing his people, she watched her uncle parade up and down.

"Tikal has proved its great strength once more," he shouted. "My brother has been defeated in battle and Dos Pilas has yielded. There is no kingdom that we cannot overthrow and no city walls that we cannot breach.

He stood tall, arms outstretched, taking in the roars of the crowd and feeding off their energy.

"My people," he continued, "the gods themselves have blessed us with great power and wealth and we will allow no others to take what is ours. Until there is no longer soil to grow our crops and sunlight to guide our path through this world, we will fight our enemies until their blood seeps into the ground and their bones lie within the dust."

He paused, turning towards Sunfire.

"Dos Pilas has given me a gift that I now present to you," he said. "My brother's son."

The crowd shrieked their approval while Brightness watched on, the sickness she felt in her churning stomach growing with every word that exited her uncle's mouth.

"My people," Dark Eyes said, lowering his arms in a gesture to calm the crowd's increasingly frenzied reactions, "there are times when a king must show mercy on those who have opposed him. My nephew has suffered enough. He has lost his father and his city has lost its prince. So long as peace remains between our two kingdoms, he will be left unharmed and free to walk within our walls as he pleases."

With that, he stopped talking, enjoying the crowd's adulation once more.

Brightness knew that it was the right time. Seeing

the guards who had accompanied her to the plaza
had become preoccupied with her uncle's speech, she
slipped between the tightly packed crowd and towards
the platform. It didn't take long for them to see that
she had escaped, but with so many people standing
shoulder to shoulder, it was difficult to keep her within
sight, her short stature an added advantage as she
was able to duck down low with greater ease than her
pursuers and squeeze between gaps that they couldn't.
She heard their angry shouts, urging people to stop her
but with all the roaring and cheering they were drowned
out. So swiftly did she move, that she managed to reach
the edge of the platform in a matter of moments, scaling
it rapidly so that she stood opposite her uncle, his
colossal frame seeming mountainous when compared
with her slender body. Breathing from her exertion and
with her legs trembling, she stood before him.

It seemed to take some time for her uncle to believe
what he was seeing, for both he and Sunfire, stood
mouths agape, their bodies seemingly paralysed.
During this standoff, the guards who'd confronted
Brightness outside the city gates had finally managed to
fight their way forwards through the crowds, they too
climbing up on to the platform. The man with the scar
on his cheek took a step towards Brightness, club raised
menacingly, only stopping in his tracks when Dark
Eyes lifted a hand dismissively. The crowds, shocked
by what had just unfolded, had fallen silent.

"People of Tikal," Dark Eyes addressed the crowd
once more, "it seems that Dos Pilas has sent us a
second royal gift. Their generosity has extended even
further than I could have wished for. I present their
princess to you."

Brightness looked down upon the mass of faces that stared back at her. This time there had not been the wild shrieks of approval that had greeted Sunfire's introduction but more of a muted muttering. They too seemed to share her uncle's surprise.

"My niece," Dark Eyes continued, "I applaud the boldness you have shown in coming here but I cannot understand why you have chosen to join your brother in Tikal. Do you have anything to say to my people?"

Brightness turned away from the crowd, staring past her uncle and locking her eyes on Sunfire's anxious face. "Trust me," she said. And although he hesitated briefly, he nodded. Summoning all the courage that she could find, she span back towards the crowd.

"People of Tikal," she said, astonished at the power of her own voice, "I stand before you today to ask for my uncle's blessing – for your blessing – right here as the gods look down upon us. Dark Eyes defeated my father in battle, and as is his right, has been rewarded for his victory with great wealth and glory. I cannot deny that he is worthy of this but I am here to beg him to change his mind and return Sunfire to Dos Pilas. Is it not enough that I have lost a father and that my mother has lost a husband? Must I lose a brother too? My uncle talks of showing mercy so let us see if he is true to his word. My brother should return home with me."

Brightness exhaled deeply and tried to control her rapid breaths while waiting for her uncle's response.

"You speak with great courage my niece," Dark Eyes said, "but what sort of king agrees the terms of peace and then allows a re-negotiation? The gods would see my weakness and punish us for it. I have to refuse. The

Prince of Dos Pilas must remain by my side in Tikal."

Brightness listened unsurprised. She hadn't truly expected her uncle to cave in to her demands.

"Very well," she said, "then under the eyes of the gods, and in their honour, I demand that a ball game is played. My brother and I will play against the twins of Tikal. If we defeat them then Sunfire is free to leave the city but if we lose then you may sacrifice our bodies to the gods and offer them our royal blood."

Hearing an audible collective gasp, she held up a clenched fist to the crowd.

"I would die for my brother," she said passionately. "This will be the greatest ball game our kingdoms have ever witnessed. Tell your king if you wish to see it."

A huge roar, enough to shake the entire plaza, rang out, not drawing to an end for some time. Adrenaline racing through her veins, Brightness stole a glance at her uncle, his face impassive and difficult to read. It didn't matter – she knew that his pride would make it impossible to dismiss her proposition. To deny his people the greatest of all ball games, and dishonour the gods in front of the temple of the two-headed serpent, would be impossible. When the crowd had eventually quietened, he gave his response.

"The game will take place when the sun rises," he said. "Your defeat will bring our city great fortune as your royal blood flows down the steps of our temple."

Chapter Fifteen

Their Blood Will Burn

Brightness awoke with the tightest of knots in her stomach. That night, she'd had to force her body to drift into sleep, ignoring the guards that stood outside her chambers, knowing that she'd need all her strength for the following day. After all, it could be her last on this Earth. She dressed slowly, pulling on her protective padding and setting her headdress in position carefully. "Have strength," she told herself softly. "If you are to die today then you will have done so having played this game as fiercely as you have ever done in your life. Do not be afraid."

She turned and walked to the entrance of the adjoining room, seeing that Sunfire was also up on his feet and readying himself. She watched as he paced up and down the room, his agitation clear to see.

"You know that you shouldn't have come here," he said, eventually catching sight of her standing there. "You'd have been safe in Dos Pilas."

"Would I?" she responded. "For how long? I heard Dark Eyes plotting to have you killed and then return to the gates of our city. He plans to burn it to the ground. How safe will I be then?"

Brightness watched her brother pressing his hands together tightly, squeezing them until his knuckles turned white.

"I knew that he would kill me one day," he said. "I knew he wouldn't keep his word. Our uncle has no honour. The priest too. They know that I can't ever forget our father's death so I knew that they'd find a way to have me killed. If not straight away, then someday soon enough, before I became a threat to them."

He rubbed his temple before continuing.

"You shouldn't have come," he repeated. "Our mother has suffered enough."

She walked to him, taking his hands in hers. "Do you think I could leave you to die? If you are to leave this Earth, then I will join you on your journey to the heavens."

He embraced her warmly.

"Thank you sister," he said.

As they took their place upon the ball court, the noise was unlike anything they'd ever heard before. Brightness had thought that she and Sunfire would receive a hostile reaction from the people of Tikal, half expecting cries of derision to ring out in deafening unison, but there was no such response. To her surprise, every step they took was cheered passionately, the crowd grateful to them for helping to provide the forthcoming spectacle, even if it may end in their grisly deaths. Louder and louder the cries became until Brightness thought that her ears may burst and despite the fear that flickered within her stomach, she couldn't deny a certain thrill at the thought of becoming the first ball game players to defeat the famous twins of Tikal. The loss that she and Sunfire had suffered against them still stung her pride and she'd always hoped for a chance to avenge it – just not when their lives depended on it. She stood, her breath escaping in rapid bursts, and tried to control herself. If she and Sunfire were to be victorious, neither of them could show any weakness.

Eventually, the crowd began to quieten and a lone

horn signalled the arrival of the pride of Tikal, its ball-playing brothers. Many believed that they were a reincarnation of the hero twins themselves, a gift from the gods to bring joy to the kingdom. However wild and frenzied the crowd had been when receiving Brightness and Sunfire onto the court was nothing compared to the rapturous welcome that now erupted. Although not identical, the physical characteristics of the ball-playing twins were very similar. Each of them was powerfully built, one being slightly taller than the other, their bare torsos both painted so that half of their upper body was covered in the black and yellow pattern of the jaguar's skin. Although they made for a fearsome sight, neither of the twins showed any of the cruelty their king displayed, playing the game fiercely but fairly, the people of Tikal loving their heroes all the more for this. Brightness watched, somewhat in awe, as they paraded around the court, gesturing to the crowd and basking in the adulation they received. She suddenly felt very small, remembering how strong and skilful her opponents had been in their previous match. It hadn't really been a close game and both she and Sunfire had been completely crestfallen at how comfortably they'd been defeated in front of their own people.

"You were younger and weaker then," she whispered to herself. "It will be different this time." However, even as the words tumbled from her mouth, she couldn't help but doubt them.

Dark Eyes, positioned in his seat that overlooked the court, rose to his feet.

"I am Dark Eyes, proud ruler of this great city," he said, "and on this day I bring to my people the greatest ball game they will ever look upon. Those of you here watching will talk of this day until the time that your final breath leaves your body. May the gods that we honour reward us for this show of faith."

He paused, letting the crowd cheer with wild enthusiasm before finally, he silenced them with a raised hand.

"My people," he said, clenching his hand into a fist, "our city must do everything to prevent being drawn into a war. I have tried to settle my differences with my brother's kingdom, both in single combat and through negotiation but still I fear that our dispute cannot be settled. This saddens me greatly for I have done everything in my power to stop further blood from being shed. On this day, I stand before the gods and honour them with a ball game that will be remembered for all of time – long after our bones have become dust. If it is the will of the Lords of the skies, my niece and nephew's royal blood will burn before the sun has fallen and further glory will be granted to our kingdom."

He stood for a moment allowing the crowd's exuberance to build, listening to them cheer for their very own hero twins. It was some time before he continued.

"As is their right," he said, "our guests from Dos Pilas should be granted a chance to speak before the game begins. Nephew," he addressed Sunfire, "On behalf of your city, do you have any words for the bold people of Tikal?"

Brightness studied her brother's face, seeing how nervous he was. Often so fearless, she hated seeing how lifeless his eyes had grown. He stood there in silence, either unwilling to speak or unable to force the words from his mouth.

"It appears that our royal guests don't have much to say," Dark Eyes said, smiling broadly. "Speak your mind nephew. I am waiting."

Brightness could hold her tongue no longer.

"My words are not for you Uncle," she said fiercely, "but for the people of Tikal and the sky lords who will watch this game. My brother and I know what we risk to try and bring peace between our kingdoms. Our blood will flow down the steps of your great temple if we are defeated but we are willing to give our lives for our city that forever lies within our hearts." Glaring up at Dark Eyes defiantly, she continued. "People of Tikal, I ask you to remember that today the gods will make their judgement. If they choose to honour my brother and I by allowing us a great victory on this court, then the quarrel between our cities is over and we should walk freely from your gates."

Locking her eyes on her uncle's, she spat out a few final words.

"May mighty Itzamn himself strike down any man or woman who defies his honour by breaking this pact. May their bodies rot in the underworld for all of time."

Chapter Sixteen

The Loneliest Climb Awaits

With the crowd's roars ringing in her ears, Brightness positioned herself at the back of the court, perspiration already sliding its way down her forehead. Pacing back and forth to her left, she saw Sunfire reach for one of the bottles of water that had been left behind the playing area. She caught his arm quickly and slipped him her own small container that she'd smuggled in and hidden within her headdress.

"Do your remember how our father weakened before our eyes?" she said and he looked back at her, his eyes quizzical.

" His xocolatl," she said. "The priest brought it to him before he fought our uncle. It would have been easy to mix in something that would dull his senses."

He stared back at her silently but there was no time for an answer as behind them Dark Eyes stood with the rubber ball within his huge hands. As the noise from those watching grew ever louder, he placed it within her grasp.

"Do you know something my niece?" he whispered to her as he drew in close, bending his giant frame down so that his face was directly in front of her own and she could smell the foul stench of his breath. "Beneath the layers of rubber that have formed this ball lies the skull of another prince who was foolish enough to challenge me. When this game is finished I may decide to make one from what's left of your brother's head. I could of course decide to choose your own. I want you to think about that every time the ball bounces upon the court."

With that, Dark Eyes turned and returned to his seat.

Fuelled by her growing anger, Brightness struck the ball with all her strength and the great game began. For an anxious moment, she thought that she had overshot the court but to her relief, she watched one of the twins move to prevent the ball hitting the ground right on the edge of the boundary line. Skidding upon the stone, he flicked out a leg and deflected the ball upwards with a padded knee while his brother moved instinctively into position. With an athletic leap, he circled backwards, surprising Brightness by turning his back on her. Swinging back his elbow, he exploded into the ball with astonishing power, sending it back across court so rapidly that Brightness only caught sight of it at the last moment, desperately flicking up her own arm to prevent her face from being obliterated. The force of the impact knocked her off her feet and she landed with a thump on the hard surface. Stunned, she recovered her senses in time to see Sunfire lunge forward and strike the ball with his knee, only meeting it with a split-second to spare, he too losing his footing in the effort made to cover the ground with the necessary speed. Before either of them could react, the twins were ready to pounce, the taller of the two reaching the ball as it floated softly up into the air, needing to do no more than help it towards the ground. Instead, he secured the point with a flourish, bending his knees and jumping high, before striking down on the ball with such strength that it not only bounced upon the court but accelerated off the stone and soared high into the crowds. It was almost comical to watch people scurry towards safety, falling over themselves in an effort to avoid being struck, the commotion only adding to the fervour of the crowd as the twins circled their half of the court whipping them into a frenzy.

Her left shin sporting a nasty graze, Brightness looked up to see her uncle applauding the skill and ruthlessness of the twins' play. On shaky legs, she rose, seeing Sunfire still lying on the ground.

"Get up," she urged her brother. "They'll slow down eventually. Stay calm and don't let them see a weakness. Even when your lungs are ready to burst don't show them that you are tired."

He nodded and they took their places at the back of the court, ready to receive the ball.

Brightness had barely had time to draw breath before the ball was hurtling towards her once more but she was ready for it, not trying to return it with any great power but directing it at an angle so that it stretched the width of the court, making the taller twin scurry across in order to cover the ground. Stretching his frame as far as he could manage, he succeeded in keeping the ball in play but could do no more than float it back in Brightness's direction, allowing her to continue to control the play. Again, she didn't make a conscious attempt to win the point quickly, but sent the ball back over the tall twin's head, not letting him rest for a moment. She heard him groan as he twisted his body sharply and backpedalled his feet as fast as he could. Once more, he reached the ball just in time but could do no more than hoist a looping, high stroke towards Sunfire. Seeing what Brightness was trying to achieve, he struck a short shot, making the same twin heave his floundering limbs forward desperately, dust flying up from the stone as his feet scraped against the surface. Controlling the flow of the game, they worked the ball from side to side, not attempting to win the point with one particular decisive shot and ignoring the jeers and catcalls from the crowd who didn't like what they were seeing. When the shorter of the twins grew frustrated at his inactivity and began to drift over and cover his brother's area of the court, Brightness sent a deep, floating shot over his head so that he too had to scurry backwards to get himself back in position. This pattern continued for some time, making it just about the longest point that she could ever remember playing, until eventually she misjudged a strike with her hip and sent the ball too close to one of her opponents. Eagerly, the taller twin accelerated into the ball with his forearm, swinging it with all his might and releasing the anger that had been building inside him as he'd been forced to turn and chase from side to side. With a thud, it struck the ground and the second point had finally been won.

Brightness watched the crowd ignite with joy, celebrating another success for their heroes. She and Sunfire were yet to score a point but when she stole a glance at the opposite side of the court, she refused to be downhearted. This time, there was no wild posturing from either of the twins, for each of them stood with their hands on hips, sucking in large breaths of air. The heat was suffocating and having to cover so much ground had caused them to suffer. Powerful and muscular though they were, this also had its disadvantages, for moving a heavy body in such humid conditions was exhausting. Brightness was sure that if she and Sunfire could keep them working then eventually they would wilt. It would be a long day, and if they could just keep the difference in points close enough, then she was sure that later in the game they would get a reward for their patience. She took a drink from her bottle and tried to control her thumping heart. No matter how much she told herself to remain strong, it was difficult to ignore the strong possibility that she could lose her life before night fell. With every shot that she took, the great temple of the two-headed serpent loomed in the background. The thought of climbing those steps after being defeated, and making the longest and loneliest of walks, filled her with a crushing dread.

Chapter Seventeen

Don't Think About The Pain

In the scorching heat, the game continued, with
Brightness and Sunfire continuing with their strategy
and working the twins into all corners of the court,
trying to make each point last for as long as possible.
When an opportunity presented itself, they would try
and take the point decisively for they couldn't risk
falling too far behind but more often than not they
would make the twins cover as much ground as they
could. As the day wore on, the twins, as expected, had
established a clear lead although it gave Brightness and
Sunfire great encouragement to see that their movement
had slowed considerably and that the gap between them
was beginning to close. Could their plan possibly work?
There was little time to think about it for if either of
them lost their concentration for a moment, the heavy
ball that thundered in their direction could smash into
their faces or their ribs and cause unthinkable damage.
Brightness remembered Flint-Knife's injury and how
he'd been unable to play properly after suffering it.
Were that to happen today, then their defeat would be
inevitable and a gruesome death would soon follow.

Diving nimbly to her left, she intercepted a strike
from the shorter twin before it hit the ground, directing
it backwards to Sunfire who hovered behind her.
Spinning her body round, she saw him aim a long,
dipping strike back over the shorter twin's head, in the
continued attempt to make him turn and run. However,
having done this so skilfully during the course of the
game, this time, he misjudged the height he put on

the ball. Brightness felt her blood rushing to her head
as she watched in horror. The loss of a single point
wouldn't matter but the line that Sunfire had taken
left the ball dangerously close to the stone ring at the
side of the court. If ever there was a temptation for
the twins to take what would be the game ending shot
then this was it, with a gentle floating ball giving them
the perfect opportunity to set their feet into position
and take their time to aim carefully. Of course, the
shot would still be incredibly difficult to make and a
failed attempt would lead to the loss of the point, but
the twins had enough of a lead to risk this. Besides, the
glory of achieving such a feat would be remembered
for eternity. Even trying the shot would make the crowd
whoop with delight.

There was nothing that Brightness could do now.
Her life was in the hands of the gods. Rooted to the
spot, she studied every small movement that the shorter
twin made, observing the way his feet shuffled into
position, watching his eyes locked on the ball, seeing
him adjust the shape of his body so that he could
direct a shot towards the stone ring high above him.
Every part of her wanted to scream at him not to do
it – to tell him that he was sentencing her to a terrible
death – to beg him to send his effort wide of the target.
Instead she remained motionless and helpless as he let
the ball drop towards his knee. He didn't try to strike
it powerfully, lifting his leg in a precise, controlled
manner to make the necessary contact. There was no
need to generate much power as accuracy was of far
greater importance. The ball whistled through the air
towards the ring of stone, the great temple lurking in
the background and the crowd taking a collective intake

of breath. Brightness blinked hard as she saw it drop narrowly below its target and land beside Sunfire's feet. She couldn't help glaring at her brother for his careless mistake and he returned her gaze sheepishly. As she took the ball from him, she saw that her hands were shaking. Even holding the ball proved difficult and embarrassingly she let it fall to the floor twice while taking up her position which led to a few derisive chuckles from the crowd. It was only when she looked up at her uncle, clearly enjoying her discomfort, that she managed to steel herself and continue play. She'd show him that she was no coward.

With the shadows growing longer and the sun beginning to fall gradually, the game moved into its latter stages. Cuts and bruises covering her body, Brightness leapt above the ball and struck down on it with her forearm. Evading the despairing dive of the shorter twin, it struck the ground hard, bouncing up and rolling right through the back of the court. The gap in the scores had grown narrower and narrower during the afternoon, with the twins tiring just as Brightness had hoped. Her latest successful strike had brought them to just one point behind and there was probably time for fifteen to twenty more plays before darkness fell and the game ended. Although her feet felt like they had been set alight and her muscles ached, she jigged about lightly on her toes as she prepared to receive the ball. When you were feeling exhausted, there was nothing worse than seeing your opponent looking fresh and ready to play all day. She wanted the twins to watch how quickly she moved and see their tired faces drop.

The ball arrived at chest height, accelerating through the air towards her. Any slight misjudgment and her sternum would be crushed. Stepping slightly to her right, she flicked out a padded hip, taking the sting out of the serve and allowing the ball to float gently above Sunfire's head. With all his remaining strength, he sprang forward powerfully, striking the ball downwards as hard as he could. The time for working the twins into the corners of the court had passed and they needed to take every chance that presented itself to them. The shot would have beaten most players but although weary, the twins of Tikal had not remained undefeated for nothing. The taller of the two brought gasps from the crowd as he reacted with incredible speed and athleticism, leaping forward to meet the ball before it struck the ground with no thought given to the pain that would shoot through his body when it thudded into the stone. Even as the skin scraped away from his sliding legs, his brother had moved forwards to meet the dropping ball, returning it back towards Sunfire at such violent speed that it became a blur of orange colour as it hurtled towards his jaw. Brightness flinched as her brother tried desperately to adjust his feet and bring his forearm up to deflect the ball, half-fearing that it would career into his face and shatter his teeth. To her relief, he somehow managed to force his defensive parry in Brightness's direction and her eyes widened as she saw the gap in which she could position a winning strike. She readied herself, heart drumming against her ribs and eyes focused firmly on the spiralling ball. It was only after she'd made contact with it, that she became aware of Sunfire still lying on the ground, seeing his stricken body through the corner of her eye, the noise of the crowd drowning out his agonised cries. Immediately, she turned towards him, vaguely registering the cheers of the crowd as her shot evaded the lunge of the shorter twin and brought the game level. As the game had progressed, she'd noticed how they'd begun to celebrate the successful shots that she and Sunfire had made, if not as raucously as those of their hero twins, but at least with a certain amount of respect.

As she reached Sunfire, he'd struggled to his feet, defiantly trying to ignore the pain that had made his face contort. Struggling to put weight on his left side, he limped to the back of the court to take a drink of water. In the effort to parry such a ferocious strike, his knee had buckled beneath him, twisting at an unnatural angle. Looking on anxiously, Brightness could already see it starting to swell.

"It's not that painful," Sunfire told her, though his grimace suggested otherwise. "We will play until the end."

He took another drink of water before attempting to retake his position on the court. It was no use. His legs gave way on him once more and he fell to one knee. Resting a comforting hand on his shoulder, Brightness crouched at his side.

"Keep still," she said. "Don't move until you are ready."

She looked over at the opposite side of the court, seeing the shorter twin with the ball in his hands. She held up the palm of her hand, motioning him to wait before turning to face her uncle.

"My brother is hurt," she said. "He will need some time to rest before we continue."

Dark Eyes looked down from his seat, his face cold as stone.

"The game will go on," he said. "It is no fault of Tikal if the boy has been hurt. I will not embarrass the gods by stopping play."

"Have the gods told you this themselves?" Brightness glowered angrily. "I do not ask for the game to be stopped, only that my brother can rest his injury for a short time. Surely the gods would not deny me that."

"The game will continue," Dark Eyes said, unmoved. "Take your positions or choose to lose the point."

Brightness looked back at Sunfire, seeing the sorrow in his eyes. He looked utterly defeated.

"You know that he will kill us whether we win the game or not," he said. "There is no way he will let us walk from his city gates. He and the priest will do as they please and twist the words of the gods to serve their own cause."

He was ready to give up and accept his fate. Brightness could almost see the fight draining out of him before her eyes. She knew that he was right though. Dark Eyes would never set them free, no matter what promises he made before the gods. She placed her hand on top of Sunfire's.

"Do you trust me?" she whispered to him.

He nodded.

"How bad is your leg?" she asked. "Do you think you could run?"

"A little. I could try," he told her. "But where would we run? A thousand arrows would be in our backs before we reached the edge of the court."

"Just trust me brother," she repeated. "When the time comes, follow me as quickly as you can. Don't think about the pain, just keep moving. Until then, don't make another move on the court. Just hold your position as best you can and leave the ball to me."

Chapter Eighteen

Stay with me

There was no time to say anything else, with the taller twin striking the ball powerfully into their half of the court, deliberately targeting the hobbling Sunfire. Although hit with great strength, the ball was close enough to him that he was able to flick it into the air without having to put any weight onto his injured knee. In a flash, Brightness was onto it, floating a shot high above the large stone ring and forcing the shorter twin into the far corner of the court. Though not a difficult strike to return, having been stretched wide, he was not able to attempt a decisive end to the point and could do no more than play a high defensive shot back towards Brightness. She didn't hesitate. Although the angle wasn't perfect, she focused her attention on the stone ring, her eyes firmly on her target. With her forearm she struck out firmly, feeling the crowd's excitement rising as they realised she was attempting the game-winning shot. As soon as she'd made contact with the ball, she was angry with herself, for the shot had been completely mistimed and sailed a long way above the stone ring. Perhaps her emotions had got the better of her and she'd put far too much power behind the strike. Her cheeks reddened as the crowd's anticipation turned to jeers of derision at such a pitiful effort. She didn't even dare sneak a look at Sunfire as she knew what he would be thinking. She was playing a game of chance with their lives. Taking on such a difficult shot was almost gifting the opposition a point.

Trying to block out the derogatory cries that rang in her ears she took the ball and prepared to serve it towards the twins.

"The Princess seems eager to place herself beneath the priest's knife as quickly as she can," a voice remarked from behind her and as much as she tried to ignore this comment, she lifted her head and stared up at the High-Priest sitting beside her uncle. A shudder ran through her body as she remembered how frightened she'd been when he'd dragged the thorns across her tongue and burnt the blood she'd shed. She knew the pleasure he'd taken from seeing her pain and could only imagine how much he'd relish the chance to take his knife and cut into her flesh – all in honour of the gods of course.

This was no time to be let her body become weakened by fear. She closed her eyes for a moment to compose herself before striking the ball deep into the opposite side of the court. Wearily forcing his legs to side-step towards the ball, grimacing from his exertions, the shorter twin met it with his hip, deflecting it towards his brother who struck it towards Sunfire. The strike was firm but from so far back there was plenty of time for him to shuffle his feet into position in readiness to meet the ball. Trying not to move his injured knee too quickly, he managed to cover the short distance without too much difficulty and, seeing an open space in which he could try and win the point, he drew back his forearm as the ball dropped slowly through the air. However, before he was able to follow through with his shot, Brightness emerged from nowhere, leaping across his path and meeting the ball with a flying knee. Again, ignoring the opportunity to

take the upper hand in the point, she aimed directly at
the stone ring, watching breathlessly and wide eyed
as it soared skywards. This time she'd controlled the
trajectory of the strike perfectly. The crowd weren't
mocking her now, their feverish yells threatening to
burst her eardrums. For all the world, the ball seemed
certain to pass through the stone hoop but with her
knee cutting across the ball slightly, Brightness had
unwittingly applied the faintest amount of spin on the
ball and at the last moment it began veering away from
the centre of the target. Striking the very bottom of the
stone ring, it fell to the ground.

Although unsuccessful, for Brightness, the strike
had served its purpose. The crowd had become more
and more raucous, both intrigued by tactics she had
adopted and exhilarated to see the game drawing close
to its conclusion. The more bloodthirsty spectators,
Brightness, thought to herself, would be looking
forward to she and Sunfire being put under the
priest's knife. It seemed to take an age before silence
eventually returned, with the taller twin waiting with
the ball in his hands. He sent a high ball towering over
Brightness's head but despite her blistered feet, she
covered the ground quickly and gracefully, turning
and flexing her hip in one fluid movement so that she
could flick a gentle pass towards Sunfire. Restricted in
his movement, he didn't attempt to return the ball into
the opposite side of the court, choosing instead to flick
the ball back in Brightness's direction. Floated softly
and angled so that it would drop slightly in front of
her, it was an ideal opportunity to take on her favourite
attacking shot once more. Bending back her right leg,
she focused her attention on the ball, meeting it with a

flying knee as it fell and sending it rocketing towards the stone ring. Again, she'd cut across it slightly, watching it start off-line before gradually arcing in towards the target. Brightness's eyes widened as she studied its path, keeping one eye on the fervent crowds who seemed to rise in one large wave. Their reaction would be crucial to her plan working. With every vein in her body pulsing, she gasped as the ball thudded into the jaws of the stone ring and ricocheted violently until all the pace had been drawn from it. Agonisingly, it teetered on the edge of the ring, seemingly unwilling to take one final roll forward. To the disbelief of all who watched, it remained perfectly still, perched up high above the court and refusing to move. By now, the crowd had lost all control, erupting with a furious roar and pushing and shoving at each other in their efforts to get a clearer view. Finally, the ball relented and toppled slowly forwards, landing in the twin's side of the court. The greatest of all ball games was over.

Brightness didn't hesitate. Wild eyed, and with a guttural roar, she leapt into the nearest section of the crowd who had already begun to step onto the court. A shot through the stone ring was a sign that the gods had given the game their blessing. It didn't matter that it had been the Princess of Dos Pilas who had achieved this feat. Desperately, they clawed at their new heroine, unwittingly scratching at her skin and knocking her headdress to the ground. Carried along in this frenzied tide of celebrations, she fought her way towards Sunfire and grabbed him by the wrist. Amongst the chaos, she managed to wrestle off his own headdress, handing it to a delighted man who sought a souvenir to take from this game. For a moment, the crowd seemed to be pulling them apart, each being dragged in opposite directions by the delirious people of Tikal, Brightness losing her grip on Sunfire for a time. Eventually, she managed to make her way back to him.

"Stay with me," she shouted, struggling to make herself heard, and staying low, they inched their way towards the edge of the court.

Their progress was slow and steady as they began trying to slip away unnoticed. As much as she tried to resist the temptation to turn her head, Brightness couldn't help turning to see how her uncle was reacting to the confusion that had spilt over the court. From the corner of her eye, she saw him barking out orders to those stood around him, rage clouding his large, rounded face. She and Sunfire didn't have much time. They'd have to move quickly but with his injured knee hindering him it was going to prove difficult. She grimaced as a stray elbow stuck her in the nose and stopped her in her tracks. As she dabbed at the thin trail of blood that trickled from her nostrils, she felt something heavy rest against her right foot. To her amazement, she saw the familiar shape of the rubber ball that just moments ago, she'd sent through the stone ring. In the wildness that had followed her winning shot, somehow, amongst the forest of legs that had swallowed up the court, it had found its way back to her. Still a little dazed, she picked it up, looking back towards her uncle once again. She had to distract him or at least slow him down somehow or his men would have them seized as soon as the crowd began to settle down. As her head cleared, an idea came to her. Dark Eyes was no more than a medium length's throw away. She was sure she could send an accurate shot in his direction. It would be far easier to pull off than aiming the ball between the stone ring, that much she could be certain of. The only thing that concerned her about this course of action was that it may alert her uncle to their position but things were so chaotic that this seemed unlikely and if she didn't do something, there was no way that they'd be able to reach the forest before they were caught. Releasing her grip on Sunfire's wrist, she steadied herself before hurling the ball in her uncle's direction, clinging on to her breath and watching anxiously as it bore down on his unprotected skull.

Dark Eyes caught sight of the missile at the very last moment, jerking back his neck and attempting to twist his head away from the heavy ball. However, he was just the slightest fraction too slow and Brightness watched his huge frame thud backwards on top of his seat as it struck him on his jaw. He didn't rise immediately, his aides flocking to their stricken king's side, their attention focused directly upon him. Within the surging crowd, Brightness and Sunfire could now lose themselves, assured that the organisation of the pursuit to capture them would be delayed at the very least. They kept their heads bowed, trying to avoid making eye contact with the streams of people that pressed against them, until finally they managed to fight their way out of the great plaza. Brightness knew they didn't have long. How badly had her uncle been hurt? It had been impossible to tell. She knew that the heavy ball had struck him and she'd seen him fall but he may just have been dazed. Once he was back on his feet, his men would scour the city in an effort to find them. Even if Dark Eyes had been badly injured then the High-Priest would soon take matters in hand and co-ordinate the search himself.

With the ball game drawing every man, woman and child to the plaza, they slipped their way through the deserted city with no guards to block their path. They too had been preoccupied with events at the courtside. Only those who stood at the city gates would still be in place for even on a day such as this, Tikal could not let its defence down completely. Knowing that she would not be able to exit the city the same way as she'd entered it, Brightness led Sunfire towards the East wall. With every laboured step that he took, she could see the pain etched upon his face but she knew that they could not stop. Not even for a moment. Taking his hand, she urged him forward until they reached the unguarded stone wall. It was much smaller than the structure that stood at the entrance to the city and in normal circumstances, they could have climbed up and over it within the blink of an eye. However, with Sunfire recoiling in pain every time he forced his wounded leg upwards, it took an uncomfortably long time before they set their feet down on the opposite side of the wall, with Brightness gently cajoling her brother through every excruciating movement, turning her head anxiously from time to time as if expecting arrows to pierce their backs as they climbed. As quickly as they could manage they inched their way towards the forest, Brightness half dragging her brother towards the trees. Her shoulders sore and heavy, she allowed herself a brief respite, breathing in air rapidly, her stomach churning all the while. Risking a glance over her shoulder, she was alarmed to see that her worst fears had been realised. Emerging from the city gates, a number of warriors made their way towards them, a hunting party of sorts, war clubs in hand and spreading out as they neared the trees so that a wider area of ground could be covered in the search that would follow. Spearheading them was her uncle, his colossal figure unmistakable.

Her mind racing, Brightness assessed her predicament. She and Sunfire had a clear head start on Dark Eyes and his band of men but with his injured knee troubling him greatly, the gap between them would soon be swallowed up. There was no possible way that they could outrun them. With no weapons and greatly outnumbered, fighting off their enemies was beyond them too. They'd be completely overpowered. She had to think smartly but quickly. Concealing themselves somehow was the only sensible option available. The jungle was extremely thick in places and she and Sunfire could possibly entangle themselves within the undergrowth until her uncle had passed. Picturing their pursuers carving through the jungle with their long, sharp blades caused her to dismiss this idea rapidly, looking up into the trees instead. Since she had been a little girl, she'd been able to make climbing look ridiculously easy, sure of foot and showing no fear of heights. It wouldn't take her long to make her way up into the very highest branches, where she could remain out of sight until her uncle and his men had passed. But what of Sunfire? There was no way he could make such a climb and she wasn't physically strong enough to haul him to safety. There had to be another way but hearing footsteps pounding the ground and drawing ever closer, she didn't have much more time to think. Then she saw it. A short distance to their left, a large tree had fallen, stretching out sorrowfully amongst the foliage.

Where it had thudded into the forest floor, Brightness could see that the ground had hollowed out, the loose twigs and leaves only partially covering the space that lay beneath. Taking Sunfire's hand, she led the way, burrowing in beside the thick tree trunk and pulling the foliage over them so they were barely visible. There they lay silently, buried alive, listening anxiously to the sound of blades cutting through their way through the trees.

Chapter Nineteen

Two Must Die

It wasn't long before Brightness heard the High-Priest's voice booming through the forest. To her horror, he seemed alarmingly close to their position.

"Your king demands that you bring back his niece and nephew alive," he shouted to the lines of men that swept their way through the jungle. "Leave no stone unturned. The gods have been denied the blood that was rightfully theirs but it must not be spilled out here amongst these trees. They must be brought back to the temple of the two-headed serpent before the sun has fallen. Only then will they be put beneath my knife."

Brightness could barely allow herself to breathe, terrified that any slight movement would alert a pursuer. Somehow, she managed to suppress the urge to cry out as a layer of soil crumbled and fell upon her face. Keeping her lips pressed tightly together so that dirt would not enter her mouth, she tried to remain as calm as possible, closing her eyes and forcing her body to remain still even as all manner of tiny creatures scurried across her motionless body. She heard the priest continue to urge his warriors forward, offering all kinds of rewards for the first man to find the escapees, his voice now so close that he must have been no more than twenty paces or so away. Her feet tucked in against Sunfire's back, she felt his body trembling. Whatever fear she felt, she knew her brother was suffering too and she hated being unable to wrap her arms around him. Together they could do no more than keep still, hope and wait.

From below the ground, Brightness could feel the
vibrations as the heavy footsteps approached. Without
being certain, she thought that alongside the priest,
there was another man, although if there was, he
remained silent and left the priest to bark out his orders.
Resisting the temptation to turn her head and steal a
glance through the foliage, she waited, terror gripping
her entire body, until she felt the figures come to a
stop beside the fallen tree, so close that she could have
reached out from her temporary prison and gripped
hold of their ankles. Feeling a trickle of sweat dripping
down from her forehead to the tip of her nose, she dug
her nails into her hands and kept her eyes shut.

"It will soon be over," she told herself. "You must
not move. They'll soon pass."

To her horror, they didn't, choosing to stand and rest
for a moment, their feet positioned perilously close to
the loose foliage. Brightness felt her stomach tighten.

"You should return to the city my King," she heard
the priest's concerned voice say. "I will bring your
niece and nephew to you as quickly as the gods will
allow it. I will put them beneath the knife before the
night has fallen."

Brightness could resist no longer, squeezing open her
eyes and blinking away the loose soil. Lying on her left
side, she was able to look up at the two men standing
above her. Though her view was restricted, she could
still make out the unmistakable figure of her uncle as
he rested alongside the priest. Squinting, she could see
that his face had sunken on one side, the right side of
his jawbone clearly broken, a result of the ball that she
had sent crashing into him. The pain must have been

excruciating.

"Your wound needs time to heal my King," the High-Priest said. "Give me the honour of continuing the search myself. I will not fail you."

Seemingly unable to speak, Dark Eyes responded with a dismissive wave of his hand. Brightness knew her uncle well enough to understand that his pride would never allow him to withdraw from this hunt. Inside, he would be raging, his broken jaw only making him all the more ill-tempered. He would not be satisfied until he had his vengeance. Yet still he didn't move, his eyes scanning the trees above him, ready to detect the slightest suspicious movement. It was as if he sensed that his niece and nephew were close but could not figure out how they remained undiscovered. He had seen the injury that Sunfire had suffered and must have known that he wouldn't be able to make their way through the forest with much haste. They must have tried to conceal themselves. But where?

Brightness closed her eyes once more, unable to bear looking at her uncle's murderous face any longer. Feeling something crawl across her face, she tried to steel herself, the speed of her breathing increasing. Terrified that it would become audible, she clamped her lips together once more, silently hoping that the gods, if they cared for her at all, would reward the courage that she'd shown. If, and she wasn't sure what she believed, her father now sat with the Lords of the skies, he would need to convince them to have mercy on her now. She felt Sunfire's body tremble once more and a surge of anxiety swept over her. How much longer could they lie in this underground tomb before one of them cracked? She wasn't sure. Her muscles, already aching after her exertions during the ball game, were beginning to cramp while she knew that if her heart raced much faster it was likely to burst. Finally, she heard feet pressing into the forest floor as her uncle and the High-Priest set off once more. Still neither she nor Sunfire dared to move, waiting patiently until finally he squeezed her hand and together they lifted their heads from beneath the ground, dirt and grime clinging to their exhausted bodies. Completely drained, they collapsed into each other's arms, hot tears streaming from Brightness's eyes. Angry at herself, she wiped them from her face. There was no time for her to cry.

Chapter Twenty

Let The Forest Take My Bones

With darkness now falling, Brightness and Sunfire moved as quickly as they could manage, cutting their way through the jungle. Choosing to veer away to their right and away from the river trail, they hoped to stay far enough away from Dark Eyes and his men and eventually swing round and head back to Dos Pilas. Although Sunfire's movement troubled him, Brightness could see his determination beginning to return as he gritted his teeth and insisted they kept moving through the night. In the morning, Dark Eyes, having failed to find them before nightfall, would likely double back on himself and have his best trackers begin the task of following their trail. They needed as big a head start as possible. With every step Brightness took, her whole body seemed to scream at her to stop and rest. Her feet, already blistered and sore from the ball game, were in a terrible state, with blood oozing from several cracks in the skin, while her head throbbed so painfully that she longed to lie down on the foliage, close her eyes, and drift into sleep. However, watching her brother ignore the pain in his injured knee and drag his battered body onwards through the forest gave her strength. Whatever pain she was experiencing was nothing in comparison to what Sunfire endured. They had to keep moving through the night. If they could reach the gates of Dos Pilas before Dark Eyes, the city would at least have a chance to repel an attack. For a moment she thought of Flint-Knife. With a day's start, he wouldn't be far from home now. She'd given him the firmest of instructions to relay to the queen. However great the urge to send an army to Tikal would be, she must resist it. Vastly outnumbered, they would be crushed by the might of Dark Eyes' warriors. The defence of the city was what mattered most, not the lives of two people. They would need every to stay behind the walls and repel any attacks with a stream of arrows. Even with superior numbers, it would not be easy for Dark Eyes to scale the walls if they prepared their defence carefully.

"Promise me you'll make my mother understand that I don't want her to send men to their deaths by trying to rescue us," she'd told him forcefully. "You must make her see that this is my wish."

He'd looked back at her with such sadness in his eyes that she'd felt the need to reassure him.

"I don't plan on dying my friend," she'd said softly. "If the gods allow it, I will return to Dos Pilas with my brother but you will give me your word before you leave."

He'd nodded and readied himself to turn and as he did so, she'd wrapped her arms around him in a warm embrace."

"Don't break your word to me my friend," she'd told him, "or I will put an arrow between your eyes myself."

They barely stopped moving throughout the night, surprised to hear the sound of raindrops drumming against the treetops. Brightness couldn't remember the last time it had rained, growing used to the sticky, suffocating heat that greeted her each morning. She listened as the faint drumming became ever louder. A fierce storm was brewing and before long loud claps of thunder burst out above them.

"The gods are angry with our uncle," Sunfire said,

126

renewed vigour in his steps.

"How do you know that it is not us they are angry with," Brightness responded, wiping her eyes.

"The storm will help remove our tracks," he told her. "It will be harder to pick up our trail. The gods are smiling upon us."

Not sure what to believe, Brightness kept her head down and kept striding forwards, brushing her sodden hair from her face. Eventually, she suggested to Sunfire that they rest, if only for a short time. Both of them were exhausted and somehow they would need to recover their strength for another big push the following day. Reluctantly, he agreed and they took shelter beneath a huge tree, huddling together for warmth and sharing a few berries that they'd managed to collect. This did little to satisfy their empty stomachs. So tired that they didn't even think about the threat of snakes or other jungle creatures, they closed their eyes and drifted into sleep.

It was some time before Brightness awoke, feeling Sunfire prodding her arm and calling her name. Groggily, she wiped the tiredness from her eyes, angry at herself for letting herself sleep longer than she had wished. Eager to get on her way once more, she stretched the stiffness from her legs, stood up, and took a mouthful of water to ease her parched throat. The storm had passed and although it had given them further opportunity to make ground on Dark Eyes, she knew that it wouldn't be long before he was on their heels. If they hurried, they could be inside the walls of Dos Pilas by nightfall. Gripping Sunfire's hand, she began sweeping through the forest once more.

With a splendid sun bursting out above them, the

night's rain began to seem like a distant memory and Brightness was grateful for its warm rays when they reached parts of the forest that weren't so dense. Even at a time like this, the beauty of the forests never failed to amaze her, with its lush green trees and brightly coloured birds always making her heart feel lighter. However, the strain of the last few days had begun to weigh heavily upon them and as the day passed, the speed of their journey grew ever slower no matter how much they cajoled each other into increasing their pace. Finally, Sunfire, who was limping more awkwardly with each step, could take no more. Crying out in pain as his leg gave way, he fell to the ground, unable to stand, even when Brightness tried to help him back to his feet."

"Every step is a step closer to home," she said, looking into his eyes and urging him to ignore his pain. "We can be inside our city before darkness but we cannot rest. Not now we have come so far."

He nodded, grimacing as he attempted to shuffle forward once more, one arm around Brightness's shoulder. It was hopeless, and falling to the floor once more, he lay on his back.

"Leave me here," he said. "I can't go any further. Let the forest take my bones."

In desperation, Brightness looked around. They were so close now, having made their way to parts of the forest that she'd grown up in. No more than a stone's throw away lay the watering hole, beside which, not so long ago, they'd caught the peccary. It was the last time they'd gone hunting with their father. What would he do in their situation?

"A great warrior isn't the strongest," he used to tell

her, "they're the one whose mind is clearest."

If ever she needed to think quickly, now was the time, for in the distance, she could hear voices. Dark Eyes and his men had caught up with them at last.

"Lift yourself onto my shoulders," she told Sunfire, kneeling at his side.

He pushed her away. "You won't be able to carry me far," he said weakly, "I'm too heavy for you."

"I won't leave you," she insisted, "and we won't be going far."

Finding strength she didn't know remained in her weakened body, she hoisted him up onto her back, staggering her way into the clearing and towards the edge of the pool.

Chapter Twenty One

Powerless

"Can you swim towards the other side?" she asked breathlessly.

"I think so," he replied. "As long as I don't kick too hard."

"Good – then wait for me there. I won't be long."

Watching Sunfire begin swimming slowly across the pool, she retraced her steps, wiping away the footprints she'd made when carrying Sunfire to the water. Then, treading down heavily to leave footprints within the mud, she headed into the forest before climbing up into the trees. Swinging through the branches, she doubled back on herself, remaining above the forest floor until she found her way back to the pool. Diving into the water, hoping to make as little splash as possible, she swam to the opposite side where Sunfire waited patiently. Lifting him onto her shoulders once more, she started to climb the steep banks in the direction of the waterfall, wary that the voices in the distance drew ever closer. Blood surging through her veins, Brightness ignored her aching muscles and cut a path higher and higher through the rocks, not daring to look down at the shimmering water below. Just one slip and they'd fall to their deaths, their bones splintering as they hurtled into the rocks that lay below the shallows of the pool. The path was now too treacherous for her to carry Sunfire any further, with overhanging branches only adding to the difficulty of the journey. Parts of the rock, eroded over the years, had crumbled in places although, having made this climb so many times, Brightness knew instinctively where to position her feet safely, following Sunfire to the edge of the fall and listening to the water thunder past her ears.

"Step through," Brightness said. "I'll be right behind you."

Watching him disappear into the cavernous space behind the waterfall, Brightness prepared to leap forward herself. Just before she did so, she stopped herself, something having caught her eye. Just above her head, barely visible against the thick trunk of an overhanging tree, was a thin, brown, papery object. Immediately, Brightness knew what it was. A hornets' nest. Looking over her shoulder, trying to ignore the huge drop, she thought quickly. Did she still have time? She hauled herself up onto the trunk, and breaking off a smaller branch, she managed to hook the nest onto the end of it. Listening to it hum angrily, she kept it at arm's length, before cautiously stepping through the water and joining her brother.

With Sunfire lying with his back against the cavern wall, totally exhausted and unable to move, Brightness stood anxiously, peering through the narrow gap in the water and observing the pool below. The first of Dark Eyes' warriors had began to seep through the trees and into the clearing, and she exhaled deeply as she watched them gather beside the water's edge, the monstrous frame of her uncle soon standing in their midst, his fury plain to see. Crouching in the mud, one of his men began to study the prints that Brightness had left but Dark Eyes clearly had little patience for this. Angrily, he shoved the tracker to the ground. Any fool could see that there were prints leading past the pool and back into the forest. Time should not be

wasted. Holding his giant right fist in the air, he urged
his men forward once more. His niece and nephew
would be close now, not far from his grasp. Brightness
looked on, her legs trembling relentlessly, as the line of
men snaked away into the trees once more. Only one
remained. Turning his head towards the pool, the High-
Priest remained unmoved, his cold eyes looking out
across the water and then back to the forest. Bending
down, he ran his fingers over one of the muddy prints
that Brightness had left before turning towards the pool
once more. He stood and walked carefully towards the
water.

From behind the pulsating torrent, Brightness could
barely bring herself to watch. Her palms sweating
profusely, she just about managed to maintain a grip
on the branch she held in her right hand, nervously
listening to the angry buzz emitted from the hornet's
nest. Beside the pool, she saw the priest begin to
scratch gently at the mud with his foot. What was going
through his mind? Would he see how she'd smoothed
over the surface and covered the tracks that led to the
pool? She shivered, her damp clothing clinging to her
aching body, the dark cavern providing her no warmth.
The priest continued to study the ground, now twisting
his head and resting his eyes upon the steep path that
led to their hiding place. An agonising wait followed
as his eyes drifted towards the waterfall, the pieces of
a puzzle beginning to come together until finally he
released a deafening cry.

Brightness felt a wave of panic wash over her.
Looking down in horror, she watched as one by one,
Dark Eyes and his warriors returned, joining the priest
at the pool's edge. Becoming ever more animated, he

began pointing across the water and up to the highest point of the path. Completely powerless, Brightness saw them begin to swim across the water and start to make the climb that she and Sunfire had done. Desperately, she stepped back into the darkness of the cavern. Was it deep enough to hide within its shadows? A wall of thick rock blocked her path and she thought again. She'd already dismissed the idea of stepping out through the water and making their escape. Sunfire could clearly no longer move and even if he could stagger his way forwards, it would take them too long to descend the path and twist away into the trees once more. Climbing the rock face would also be impossible. Away from the path, the rock was slippery and treacherous. Anyone who was foolish enough to attempt such a feat would surely fall to their deaths within moments.

Perhaps Brightness thought to herself, "this would be preferable to the death that awaited them within the temples of Tikal. At least it would deny her uncle the satisfaction of having them put beneath the priest's knife.

She returned to the edge of the cavern, a splitting pain within her head emerging as she saw Dark Eyes and the High-Priest leading a long line of warriors towards them. Closer and closer they moved, inch by inch, until the path became so narrow and perilous that they pushed themselves back against the rock, wary of the certain death that would await them if they took one false step. Her breath imprisoned within her throat, Brightness watched them snake their way steadily forwards, eyes focused on the eroded path, taking the utmost care with every movement. There was nothing she could do but wait.

Seeing her uncle's menacing frame standing just beyond the cascading water, Brightness summoned the last drop of defiance that boiled within her.

"I am armed," she yelled, trying to repel the fear she heard in her own voice. "My spear will rip through the throat of the first man who steps through the water."

Dark Eyes stopped. There was only room for one man at a time to step from the ledge and into the cavern. Only a fool would refuse to show caution.

"My niece," he said, having to force the words from his shattered jaw, "I know you speak falsely. You have no such weapon. You would be wise to accept your situation and place yourself in my hands."

Her anger rising, Brightness refused to back down.

"Why would I do that uncle? So that my blood can cover the steps of your great temple. My brother's too. Do you plan to tell your people that this was the will of the gods?"

"You must stand before them," Dark Eyes said. "Your actions on the ball court dishonoured them. Even you must see that my niece."

"The gods will reward my brother and I for our victory," Brightness responded. "They have guided us this far. If you choose to break the vows you made before them, then I am certain that they will punish you without mercy. Return to Tikal immediately and they may choose to spare you."

Even through the blur of the thundering water, Brightness could see her uncle bristle with anger.

"The time for talk is over," he said furiously. "Step out and hand yourselves to me or I will ensure you will suffer before you die. You will beg me to slide my knife across your throats and bring your pain to an end."

Brightness shivered inwardly, her legs threatening to collapse beneath her. She was so exhausted now, her eyes heavy and sore, the fight slowly draining out of her. She just wanted it all to end. All this hatred and violence.

"Do I have your word that my brother and I will receive a quick death?" she said sorrowfully.

"I vow to you that I will be merciful," Dark Eyes replied.

"Then step back Uncle," Brightness announced. "Step back, for I am ready."

She looked down at Sunfire who lay in the darkness. He looked utterly defeated, his eyes barely remaining open, his head tilted to one side.

"I love you brother," she told him. "Rest your eyes."

Balancing the hornet's nest on the end of the branch she held, she called out to Dark Eyes.

"Leave room for me on the path uncle," she said. "I am right here."

She heard Dark Eyes instruct his men to inch backwards as carefully as they could, and her head pulsing violently, she prepared herself for what she must do. The nest was now vibrating angrily, the first hornets beginning to emerge. She winced as she felt one sink its sting into her shoulder, the venom entering her bloodstream. Ignoring the pain, she sprang from the water, landing on the narrow path and twisting her body towards her tormentors. She saw the shock on her uncle's face as she launched the hornets at his chest, watching as the seething swarm of insects exploded from the nest, smothering Dark Eyes' head and torso. Brightness stood back, watching the chaos

unfold before her eyes, her uncle's violent screams
ringing in her ears. His giant arms began flailing out in
a desperate effort to fend off his attackers but in doing
so his right foot slipped from the path. Disorientated,
he reached out and clawed at the High-Priest who stood
behind him, he too plagued by the relentless swarm.
For a moment it seemed like Dark Eyes had managed
to steady himself, but as he and the priest stumbled
backwards clumsily, the eroded path collapsed beneath
them. Brightness watched them fall, along with the two
nearest warriors to them, their anguished cries hanging
in the air until their bodies struck the rocks below with
a sickening crack. Averting her eyes at the last moment,
she tried to control herself. A large part of the path had
broken away, leaving a gap that was too far to jump.
For now, she and Sunfire were safe. Looking across
at what remained of Dark Eyes' men, she saw that at
least twenty warriors remained, many of their faces
already red and puffy from hornet stings. The insects
were now dispersing, and the men left on the path were
now regrouping into some sort of order. At the very last
moment, Brightness saw a gleaming blade whistling
towards her just in time, leaping to her right and back
into the sanctuary of the cavern. Gasping for air, she
resumed her position behind the water, defenceless
now, watching for her pursuers' next move.

With Dark Eyes and the priest having fallen to their
deaths, it was difficult to see which of the warriors was
now taking command. Between them, some sort of
order seemed to be being relayed along the line and the
two men who brought up the rear began making their
way back down towards the pool and into the forest.
It seemed to take an age before they reappeared once

more, carrying a small but solid piece of wood they'd cut from a tree. Cautiously, taking the utmost care with every step, they began to make the journey back up the steep incline. Watching on as the two warriors at the forefront of the line drew long knives from their belts, Brightness's heart began beating rapidly once more. For a moment, she thought they would hurl themselves through the water and into the cavern and she made sure that she kept her head tucked tightly behind the rock. Slowly, the line of men passed the trunk along until it reached the front. Putting their knives away, the two leaders took the trunk and carefully began to position it so that it bridged the gap to the cavern. Panic rising within her chest, Brightness considered her options. She thought about leaping out from behind the water once more and kicking the trunk away but this didn't seem like a risk worth taking. She could see that many of the warriors held their knives aloft, ready to sink them into her flesh in an instant. It wouldn't matter how quickly she moved, at least one blade would find its target. But what else could she do? Quickly, she looked around the cavern. There were a number of small pieces of rock lying about and, keeping one eye on the warriors outside, she selected two that were suitable to throw at anyone beginning to cross the bridge. At the very least it may deter the warriors from approaching, for crossing the trunk would be dangerous enough without having to evade missiles. Lying broken on the rocks below, the body of their king was a reminder of what would happen if they were to lose balance and fall.

As the first man tentatively set foot upon the trunk, Brightness took aim and sent a piece of rock hurtling in his direction. Her fingers cold and slippery, she misjudged her throw slightly and the rock took just a glancing blow of the first warrior's shoulder. This only seemed to increase his determination, his eyes narrow and fierce. Brightness had one more chance. She couldn't afford to waste it as there would be no time to retrieve any more rocks. With every last drop of her energy she flung her missile towards the bridge, barely able to watch to see if it would save her. This time her aim was truer but the element of surprise had been lost. Leaning his head skilfully to one side, the warrior evaded the rock and it sailed through the air, making its way towards the pool below. Brightness felt her heart sink along with the rock as it struck the water, the fight slipping out of her body. The first warrior had now reached the end of the makeshift bridge, a second also ready to make his way across. She stood on trembling legs, resigned to her fate, watching the warrior step from the trunk and onto the path. Just one step forward into the rushing water and he'd enter the cavern. Would he draw his knife and cut her throat or would she and Sunfire be taken back to Tikal and paraded as a prize? Did it matter? Either way they'd be killed. However, before another thought could enter her head, Brightness saw an arrow thud into the trunk, missing the warrior who stood on the path by inches. A second soon followed, stopping him in his tracks, not daring to move a muscle. A familiar voice rang out from below.

"Lay down your blades," her mother called out. "Cast your weapons aside and your blood will not be spilt."

Not one of the warriors moved and another arrow thudded into the tree trunk.

"The next arrow will pierce flesh and not wood," the Queen continued. "There are thirty archers that stand beside me. I urge you once more to throw your weapons into the water. You have my word that your lives will be spared."

Still, there was no movement and Brightness found herself holding her breath.

"I will not ask again," the Queen continued. "I will protect my family if I must but I repeat that I do not seek further death. Your king has passed to the underworld and the quarrel between our cities ends here. Return to Tikal with my blessing and in time we will may see each other as allies once more."

Peering around the falling water, Brightness saw the warrior, who stood before her, turn towards her mother and the archers of Dos Pilas, slowly releasing his grip on his knife and throwing it into the still water. Taking his lead, the others soon followed his action, before silently, this line of fearsome men, began to make their way back down the path. When they reached the water's edge, they didn't swim back across the pool, but slipped away into the forests and disappeared from view. The war, at least for now, was over.

It wasn't long before Brightness began helping Sunfire back towards the pool, every step slow and painful. Eventually, they managed to make their way across the cool water and collapsed into their mother's arms. Salty tears now streaming down her grime covered face, Brightness became aware of a familiar figure standing to her left.

"Flint-Knife!" she said, her face registering surprise as he handed her a bow.

"I broke my promise to you Princess," he said. "You

may place an arrow between my eyes."

Lost for words, Brightness hugged him.

"I will think of a different punishment someday," she whispered smiling. "Maybe not death – but something really bad."

They both laughed and walking towards the trees, they prepared to make the short journey back to Dos Pilas. Just before entering the forest, she turned to look back at the pool at which she'd spent so much time with her father, exploring, hunting, learning to use a bow. Then she saw it, above the waterfall, soaring gracefully up into the skies. A proud eagle, flying so high that its wings could brush against the heavens themselves. Her heart fluttering, she watched it soar.

Scoring for the Stasi

In East Germany in the 1960s, football mad Karl wants nothing more than to play for his hometown club. However, when this dream finally comes true, he soon finds out that playing for the mighty Dynamo Berlin comes at a cost. Karl realises that the team are run by the dreaded Stasi Police and he's required to be more than just a football player. And players don't leave Dynamo Berlin until the Stasi decide.

ISBN: 9781906132453   **£7.99**

The Wartime Winger

*"Imagine it Jim - champions of the world.
That'd be alright, wouldn't it?"*

Growing up in the North of England in the 1930s, Jimmy Evans and his best friend Stan share a burning ambition to play for England in the World Cup. After years of hard work, and against the odds, it seems like their dream may even come true as they are tipped for a call up to the national team. However, a terrible new war is brewing. When Jimmy and Stan are finally asked to represent their country, it will be in the skies of Europe and not on the football pitch!

ISBN: 9781906132156   **£7.99**